ALIEN VIRUS LOVE DISASTER

ALIEN VIRUS LOVE DISASTER

STORIES

BY

ABBEY MEI OTIS

Small Beer Press
Easthampton, MA

This is a work of fiction. All characters and events portrayed in this book are either fictitious or used fictitiously.

Small Beer Press
150 Pleasant Street #306
Easthampton, MA 01027
smallbeerpress.com
weightlessbooks.com
info@smallbeerpress.com

Distributed to the trade by Consortium.

Library of Congress Cataloging-in-Publication Data

Names: Otis, Abbey Mei, 1989- author.
Title: Alien virus love disaster : stories / Abbey Mei Otis.
Description: First edition. | Easthampton, MA : Small Beer Press, [2018]
Identifiers: LCCN 2017047745 (print) | LCCN 2017048481 (ebook) | ISBN 9781618731500 | ISBN 9781618731494 (alk. paper)
Classification: LCC PS3615.T55 (ebook) | LCC PS3615.T55 A6 2018 (print) | DDC 813/.6--dc23
LC record available at https://lccn.loc.gov/2017047745

First edition 1 2 3 4 5 6 7 8 9

Set in Bembo 12 pt.

Printed on 50# Natures Natural 30% PCR recycled paper by the Maple Press in York, PA.

Contents

To the teachers,
all of you,
& especially mine.

Alien Virus Love Disaster

What happens first is people in hospital masks come banging on our doors before it's even light out. They herd us out of our houses and down the block to what used to be the football field of Paige Clifton Senior High School. They make us strip and pile our clothes on the bleachers. It's August but the mist hasn't burned off the morning yet and we shiver. Especially Mrs. Todd shivers, who's eighty-two. There's like two hundred of us, everybody who lives on James Row plus 12th Street plus whoever they could prod out of the Amorcito apartments. Megaphones all over blaring *state of emergency, please proceed in an orderly manner, this is a matter of public safety.*

They push us naked into the field.

Near me are the Naylors who never come out of their corner house, the Sherman sisters I've known all my life, Trini with her baby who always cries but is dead quiet now. People hunch like peeled shrimp with giant scared eyes. "Man, what is this bullshit?" asks Dean, my little brother, he's twelve and I should smack him for that kind of language but that's when they turn the fire hoses on us.

Everyone lifted off their feet, everyone hurled into everyone else. Legs hair ribs nails. Mrs. Todd folds in half. Dean goes facedown so hard his nose snaps on the mud. I want to scream but I think if I opened my mouth I'd be filled with water, windsock-in-a-hurricane style. Somebody's wet foot tangles with my shin and I smack down into the wet earth. Mouthful of torn-up grass and grit and slime. I roll over. Lying on my back I can see past the wreck of water and bodies. Way above us the sun's coming up. The rising spume fills the sky with rainbows. On a normal day I'd be awake by now. I'd be about to take a shower.

People stumble down next to me, over me. The hoses blast away everything, dirt, skin, memory. I'm starting to disintegrate just like the earth. My brain is going to mingle with the soup. Bye Trini, bye baby, bye Dean, you were so right, what is this bullshit? I for sure don't know.

The hoses go off.

Your clothing will be incinerated, the megaphone says. *You can fill out a form for compensation from the Office of Toxin Containment. You'll get an information packet detailing Follow-Up Action in seven to ten business days.*

We're all shaky trying to get out of the muck. People pull on each other to stand and slip and drag someone else down with them. Everybody's got a painted camo warrior face and some of us have red streaks where our noses bled or our skin flayed away. Someone is like, "Well, guess we better get cleaned up," and someone else has the balls to laugh.

. . . .

Where Dean and I live is the downstairs left side of a fourplex with linoleum floors even in the bedroom. They call it a fourplex but really it's five because they put some plywood around the water heater in the basement and rented the extra space out to an immigrant family. The only window they have down there is the hole in our kitchen floor where sometimes I peek through and see them all clustered around a hot plate. What's in front is weeds and the spot where Mrs. Todd couldn't get any squash to grow and a Jobs With Justice sign some little guy came by and stuck in the yard five years ago. What's in back is kind of a deck but the boards are sagging in the middle so it's shaped like a U. You might think there's more weeds under the deck but wrong: just concrete. And beyond the concrete there's some chain link and beyond the chain link there's this enormous dirt field and way out in the middle of the dirt is the low-down gray building everybody calls the Magic Factory.

Why it's called that is because that place puts on better shows than Fourth of July, I'm serious. Fourth of July only might be better because you always know when it's coming: right after the third, duh. Magic Factory shows are always a surprise but once it gets going somebody will yell and then everybody comes out to watch. The Sherman sisters have a whole set up with folding chairs but mostly people just stand in their backyards or press faces to the chain link or climb it if they've got tiny feet. (You can't climb all the way over because of the razor wire.) Back when Mom lived with us and Benning was sniffing after her, he'd lift me or Dean up on his shoulders so we could see better. The best thing was when someone was doing a cookout the same night as a Magic Factory show. Like you're chomping down, boiling hotdog juice squirting into your mouth, and then you look over and there's glitter pouring out of the smokestacks on top of the building. I say glitter but every time is different. Sometimes big spreads of color that hover over the roof pulsing like heartbeats. Or sometimes just rivers of stars gushing up and up and spreading across the night and then falling. You clamp your hotdog in your mouth and stretch out your arms but just when the stars are about to land on your wrists they disappear, they always disappear.

Or sometimes you'll be picking corn out of your teeth and suddenly the air is full of sound. Like music but no tune and no words so maybe not like music. Always it's way too loud to talk over and it kind of hurts your ears, but also it kind of hurts your heart in a way I think everybody secretly enjoys. Like the most beautiful animal in the world is trapped in a cage somewhere inside there. And we are the ones who have to listen to it, and we are the ones who get to listen to it.

The day after they hose us down there's a bunch of caution tape wrapped around the Magic Factory. And down on Marion Street there's a big padlock on the gate that leads into the dirt field. The sign that said Property of the Federal Government, No Trespassing is gone and now there's just one that says Decommissioned. I'm going to be honest there's definitely no geniuses living on this block, but you don't need to be a genius to figure out everyone who got hosed lives in a house that backs up against the Factory. I think probably you could even be a little, I know I'm not supposed to use this word but, retarded, and still make something of that.

. . . .

What happens next is an email comes with a list of drug prescriptions and a pharmacy voucher for fifty bucks. *Consumers in the listed neighborhoods may have come into contact with dispersed agents (see notification 103C). The following regimen is recommended, however has not been endorsed by the FDA.*

At the drug store the pills come to sixty-four forty so I start counting out change.

"You got a day off for these?" The drug-store lady taps a bottle.

"What's that?"

"This one's gonna keep you at home for a day. How come everybody's asking for these? Tell you what I don't envy none of you one bit."

"Like what do you mean?"

"You got a question you call the number. Number's on the receipt."

"What—"

"Sweetheart there's a long line behind you." She points and it's true. Old man and lady and a woman with a baby on each hip and everybody's clutching their printed-out voucher.

So I'm walking out past them and I get this idea to be like, "Oh I think I remember you from somewhere? You were the one all muddy and screaming? Maybe you remember me, I was all muddy and screaming too?" But nobody laughs.

Little brother is on the sofa when I get back to the apartment.

"Oh Dean I know you did not get sent home the first day of school."

He rolls his eyes because obviously. "Mrs. Shipley lied. Mrs. Shipley said I was in the hall after bell but she saw me coming and she shut the door early. She slammed it in my face. Why does she hate me so bad?"

"You need to quit the excuses and start the explainings. Like now."

"What she said was I was banging on the door threatening her. Like yeah Mrs. Shipley you think I care about your dumbass study hall? Like shit. She hates me."

"I'm serious if you swear one more time . . . She doesn't hate you. You're making trouble for yourself."

Instead of listening he gathers his limbs together in a gangly bouquet. He digs at the sole of his bare foot, peels off a big nugget of callus and flicks it onto the rug.

"Omigod Dean gross pick it up pick it up!" I smack his head with the bag of pills and he skitters into the bathroom.

Now I'm alone. The room is still. The basement family isn't rustling around. Late afternoon sun turns everything gold, even the dead skin crumbs on the floor. I line up the pill bottles on the table. They all have long names full of Xs and Zs, and I know that's how you trust something's authorized scientific but it still makes me kind of nervous. The labels say something about don't take on an empty stomach so I put two patties in the microwave. "Dean? Come out here. You got to take some of these." He doesn't answer so I count out pills for myself, line them up in my hand. Little blue moons, pink circles, orange-and-white ovals. One deep breath then they all go down together. I wash them down with red juice out of the bottle, so sweet I kind of stop being able to breathe for a moment.

"Dean? Seriously come here."

The bathroom door stays closed.

. . . .

There's too much to do in the mornings. There's do we still have enough minutes on the prepaid, is there enough money left in checking, where's the credit card, the other credit card, does Dean have his bus pass, backpack, shoes, homework. There's has anyone messaged for a nail appointment, because don't laugh but I'm still hoping this small-business thing will take off. I can do all these things at once, I'm a multitasker like that, but it's a dance, if I get messed up I can't start again.

What happens this morning is, right in the middle of counting out a dollar for Dean: pain. No-joke pain. Like someone tangled their hand deep in my guts and yanked. I shriek in Dean's face and his hand that was held out for a nickel instead gets a big gob of my spit.

"The hell, big sister?" But I can't do anything except double over and make noises like someone's pulling saws out of my throat. There's a fat python clenched around my insides. There's a cat hanging by its claws from between my legs. I shriek and shudder again and see Dean staring at me, mouth open, still cupping my spit in his palm.

"Noma—are you—?"

He looks younger when he's afraid. There's a seeping warmth in my underwear and I'm pretty sure I don't want his help on this one.

"It's okay. Get out of the way."

Somehow I get into the bathroom and pull my jeans down and wow is my underwear a mess. Rust and pink and bright red jelly down my legs. All I can do is collapse on the toilet and hunch over my knees. The pain rolls through in spurts and I bite the heel of my hand so Dean won't hear me yell. Spit slicks down my wrist.

I wrench my brain away from panic and try to get my breath to slow down. Blue light filters down from the high-up window. There's the plink plink of the sink leaking and the sigh of the toilet tank and no other sounds. It smells like how I imagine a cave smells. I lay my forehead on my knees and peer between my legs. The cramps turn everything blurry like Vaseline smeared on a camera lens. Every task I was trying to finish falls away. Nothing to do except inhale, exhale, and watch the blood fall out of me in ropes.

When Dean inches open the bathroom door and peeks around I'm in a numb ball on the tile, pants still around my ankles. He puts his hands in my armpits and lifts me like a child.

"Dean? You missed school?"

He doesn't say anything. He gets a washcloth and runs the water until it warms. He gathers up my ruined clothes and carries them away.

I sit in the tub until I stop shaking. Then I tell Dean to go get the bottles on the table. He still doesn't speak.

"Just pour them in the toilet."

He doesn't ask why. The toilet bowl is scattered with pastel constellations. I think about how such tiny things can have such long names. I think about the constellations that rose out of the Magic Factory. I think about the spray from the fire hoses that made bruises on our bodies and rainbows on the sky. I push the lever and the toilet glugs and everything disappears.

. . . .

"Like hell I took them."

Trini and Trini's cousin and Georgia Sherman and I sit on Georgia's front porch, and I'm working on Trini's cousin's nail beds. Trini's joggling her baby on her knee and explaining why she didn't take her pills. "He's still nursing, you know? Like I'm all about natural weaning. And I don't ingest nothing unless my doctor says. And you know my doctor hasn't called me back in a year, so." She clicks her tongue and shrugs.

I'm thinking come on Trini, you were feeding that baby chicken poppers before he had teeth. But I like that she's with me on the pill thing so I just keep pushing her cousin's cuticles.

"Well I took them." Georgia says it in her I'm-old-and-I-don't-have-time-for-this voice. "Just to be on the safe side. They still won't even say what happened to us. I think I'm having a reaction, though. I got this spot." She pulls up her shirt. Above her hip there's a red bump wide as a quarter. Trini is going "Uh, yeah, what'd I tell you?" but then she looks and goes "Oh. But I—I got one like that."

Hers is on the small of her back, to the right of her spine. "That is so weird, you know?"

I stop in the middle of applying a base coat and ask can I touch them. The bumps feel hard and round like everybody's got ping-pong balls buried inside them. Trini giggles. "Dang Noma your fingers are *ticklish*."

Then I lift up my shirt and show them the three bumps on my stomach and Trini stops giggling. "Oh what. Oh what the. Oh wow."

Trini's cousin is from the coast and she's looking at us like she doesn't even want to know what's going on in this neighborhood. I reach out to finish putting on her enamel and she hesitates before giving me her hand.

The sun is going down and painting the sky so pretty someone should put it in a museum. I make each of that cousin's nails disappear under three strokes of Copper Wildfire. Nobody gets up to go into the backyard. Nobody looks for magic shows anymore. We never said anything about it to each other but we all just know.

So like you expect a lot of things to be hard in life. Like there will always be bills and always landlords and your mom's always gonna be running off with creepy boyfriends and fake friends are always gonna be stabbing you in the back. Like even when you get fired from the nail salon where you've worked for two years and you weren't even ever late except that one time, even that isn't too surprising. But having weird bumps sprouting up all over your body, and now there's way more and they're growing bigger—that's the kind of thing you just don't really plan for.

At this point I have nine and Dean has fourteen. I don't know how many other people have because it would be weird to go around counting but I'm sure it's a bunch. Hardly anybody sits outside on James Row anymore. Dean's quit making up excuses for skipping school. I'm supposed to be mad about that but it's like the mad part of me has shriveled up and blown away. Instead this afternoon I'm like let's treat ourselves, why not. We walk down to the carry-out by the highway and get shrimp fried rice and wings and crazy fries and we don't even wait to get back to the house to start eating. We shovel orange rice into our mouths with our hands.

Dean wipes his fingers on his shirt and rubs the lump swelling on his neck. Then he drops his hands to his sides and stares out at the eighteen-wheelers charging down the highway. "Nothing like this has ever happened before."

His voice is so empty that I swallow a whole shrimp without chewing at all. I keep coughing for longer than I need to because I'm trying to figure out what to say back.

"Hey. You don't know that. Maybe there's some fancy doctor somewhere and all he does is study this. Maybe we find him and he fixes us."

Dean doesn't look away from the highway. "Seriously, big sister? You think I got lumps on my brain?"

"You shut up. I was just trying to think positive or something. I don't know."

We finish the fried rice without speaking. We start on the crazy fries. So many cars fly by. I wonder what would they think if they slowed down to look at us. If they saw what was under our clothes.

"Naw," Dean goes, "This is something new. We got to start thinking totally different about this."

"Different like putting a fry in your nose?"

"What?" But he's too distracted and I get one in each of his nostrils before he can duck, and then it's just like when he was six and I was twelve and he's yelling "Fry monster, fry monster!" and chasing me all the way home.

I lose him going up the hill, he's still faster even with fourteen lumps, and so I'm walking and huffing toward home when I see a car parked on the corner of James Row and Marion Street.

Little hatchback, shiny red like a toy, no exhaust pipe—nobody around here owns one of those cars. I stare at it for a moment but then Dean is yelling for me to come unlock the door, so I go on.

For a while Trini had this guy friend but now he says he's not going to come around anymore. Just to be safe, he says.

"What a useless coward, you know?" Trini holds both her eyes open with her fingers. "No way am I going to cry over him."

I pull her hands away from her eyes. I get out my little soak tub and set her fingers in hot water. "Honestly I think you're kind of lucky. Like if I was betting on which of you was going to be giving out diseases, I would not put my money on you. Just saying."

"What is that, supposed to make me feel better?"

"Yeah."

"You know what Noma? You are pretty cold sometimes." She's tipped way forward on the couch because by now the lumps are all over her back like little mountains. "That coward said it was his 'survival instinct,'" she goes on. "Said I couldn't blame him for just following his survival instinct."

The baby sits on the floor in front of her. He's got just this one lump between his shoulder blades. It makes it look like maybe he's about to sprout wings. I lift Trini's hands from the soak and start to massage her wrists. I work my way over the tendons in the back of her hand, feel them shift over her bones. I'm standing up because the lumps make it hard for me to bend in the middle. Our skin is stretched shiny in the places where the domes grow. Sometimes I think I can feel them rasping against each other inside me.

"They're kinda like elegant, you know?" Trini says. "Like better than some tattoo or something. And, I'm serious, way better than being pregnant. No offense baby." She tickles the baby who breathes funny now that his lump is basically as wide as his whole back. I rub moisturizer into Trini's knuckles, knead each of her fingers, our hands are fragrant with cucumber-melon. Then without really thinking I reach up and stroke the lump below her shoulder. Her skin slides just a little bit over the hardness. I imagine them all hidden in the darkness of her, baseball-sized diamonds buried in black earth. White hot lumps of star stuff buried in black space.

Now that I've seen it once I see it every day, that little red car parked on Marion Street. This time it's right by the taped-up Magic Factory gate, and through the back windshield I notice a silhouette in the driver's seat, upright and still.

I walk up along the sidewalk and tap on the passenger window. "What you still doing here?"

Inside there's a man looking like a lawn gone to seed. Wrinkled dress shirt done up wrong and stubble patching his jaw. His head jerks when I knock. "Huh?"

"Yeah, huh. What are you still doing here?"

His eyes are big and dark as holes and his mouth works soundlessly.

"What, you can't hear me? How about you open the window?"

Long hesitation and then, without taking his eyes off me, he raises his hand and toggles the window down.

"That's better. Look I was just curious, I guess. What are you doing here?"

"I'm sorry." He brings a thumb to his mouth and gnaws on the nail. He still hasn't blinked. "I don't know what you're talking about."

"You worked in there." I jerk a thumb at the Magic Factory. "I used to see your car go in. Plus my girl Trini was first-shift security guard, that little booth right there. But you know, it's closed now. *So why are you still here?*"

He so slowly raises his hands, turns them palm up like he's about to receive a present from the steering wheel. Then he methodically, mechanically lowers his face into those palms.

I hold on to the door rim and use one big toenail to scratch an itch on my other ankle. I wait.

He slides his hands down an inch. "I don't know. I ask myself. I can't—I can't seem to let it go."

"What's *it?*"

"I was a researcher. I was helping to—" Then his eyes change like he's remembering other things about me, "But you know already. You must have seen."

"We saw the magic shows, yeah." I put my elbows down on the door rim and lean through the window into his car. "Tell me."

He starts to laugh. "It's all gone! Poof! I never worked here. Your memory must be tricking you. Check the records, there was never even a lab."

He's not really getting it. "Research-man I don't have a lot of time." I lean farther into his car and smell the unwashed smell. "You didn't call it magic show, I bet."

"We had longer words. We thought that meant we understood it better."

"But you didn't."

"No."

"You didn't know shit."

He reaches for my face, stops his hand halfway across the distance between us. "Look at you. It glows inside you. Even I can see that."

His dark hole eyes widen like he wants to take in every inch of me. I try to imagine him in lab coat, ironed, clean-shaven. Probably at one point he was the kind of person I'd be scared to talk to, which almost makes me laugh. Like imagine you spend your whole life afraid to look on the face of God, and then you finally do and it turns out he's just one more eyes-nose-mouth combo, just another blur to be learned in a minute, remembered or forgotten without much work.

Instead I hiss, "If I dragged you out the car right now and stomped your head into the curb, would you fight me?"

He shakes his head and I can hear small dry things rattling in his hollow body. "No."

"Would it change anything?"

His eyes meet mine and between us we hold the answer unspoken.

"Why don't you leave us alone, then? You didn't before. You could now."

He flinches. "I—I wanted you to know. I had to tell someone. For whatever it's worth. I'm sorry. It was a mistake. I'm so sorry."

I don't really sleep anymore. Kind of I just lie in bed and sweat and imagine shapes in the dark. Once in the deepest part of the night I hear a weird noise coming from the front of the house. A shivery kind of croon. I coax the orbs of my body into a standing position and feel my way to the living room. Dean sits up on the sofabed, shaking. I turn the lamp on and see his face shiny with tears.

"Little brother? You okay?"

He can barely get out words between sobs. "It was—just a dream."

I haven't seen him cry so hard since he was three. "Aw, shh. That's right. Just a nightmare. It's gone now."

He's still crying but he manages to shake his head. "It—it wasn't—wasn't a nightmare."

"Oh yeah? What was it?"

"It was—so beautiful."

"Oh. Well, like, that's not so bad then, huh? What was beautiful?"

He snorks a big load of snot back into his head. Wipes his face on the edge of my T-shirt. "The things—the things that are growing in us. That are getting ready to come out."

And it's like all my insides have vanished, which is good because otherwise I might throw up. "But I didn't—but I never said—"

His sobs have stopped and now he's just laughing really quiet. "Noma I wish you'd quit acting like I'm in diapers. It won't do you any good. Everybody can feel it. We're the Magic Factories now."

Next morning Dean is gone. He spends most of his time now by the dumpster outside the Amorcito Apartments, passing roaches around with high-rise delinquents. I always thought those kids were kind of dead in the eyes but whatever, I guess so are we. I walk down there and find him laying into this pale kid with more lumps than anyone I've seen.

"What are you, sad? You think this is some kind of therapy session?" Dean kicks the dumpster to punctuate his sentences. "There isn't a thing to be sad about. There's never been anything like us. We're the next stage. The whole world is going to pay attention."

The wispy kid has a hard time stringing together a response. "I know. It's just. It's scary. Sometimes. When you think about it."

"Scary?" Dean's voice goes all smooth. "I know. But you can't be scared either. You have to welcome it. Think how pretty a butterfly is." I get shivers listening to him talking like an adult while his voice still seesaws between high and low. His voice that used to beg me to go to the splash park or call me over to look at some weird bug he'd found. He's almost six feet tall now though he doesn't look it. Just a jumble of elbows and shins and Adam's apple and hair that hasn't been washed in too long. It makes his lumps stand out even more. Now he reaches out and strokes the kid's bumpy head. "When you see the butterfly, you understand why the cocoon rejoices as it breaks."

Rejoices as it breaks, rejoices as it breaks, I start walking and the words churn around my brain, faster and faster as my steps speed up. I see the little red car parked by the lab gate and I head straight for it, blood rough in my ears. The passenger-side door is unlocked, of course it's unlocked, and I get in and slam it behind me. I stare straight ahead. Outside the sun is going down and the sky is a smooth creamsicle field.

After a moment he says, "Is something happening? Do you feel different?"

Yeah I knew he'd ask this, and I wanted him to, except now it only pisses me off. Out the corner of my eye his hands are folded in his lap; he scrapes the cuticle of one thumb with the nail of the other.

"Can you describe the sensations in your torso right now?"

Now I look at him. "You're serious?"

"If you can tell me what you're experiencing, I might be able to get some sense of the progression of—"

"Jesus, mister scientist man, I don't fuckin know." I kick my sandals off and arrange my feet on his dashboard. "How about you drive already?"

He is still and silent for a moment, then he pushes the ignition. The car hums to life quieter than an electric razor. In the side mirror the Magic Factory slides away behind us. I don't say anything until we're coming down the ramp onto the highway. "You want to know how I'm feeling? I'm feeling like I want to see someplace pretty. You know anywhere like that? Take me someplace really fuckin pretty."

We stand on the edge of a river. The water is cloudy and clogged with floating islands of sticks and muck and lost flip-flops. On the far bank the sunset licks the trees with copper. I exhale and feel something more than air flow out of me.

The scientist grazes my wrist with his bitten-up fingernails. "They found it near here, you know. In a field. Not far away. Not out in space. It fell right here. And we thought we were so lucky—we got to name it. We got to do something wonderful for humanity. We weren't bad people." He twists toward me. "If you had the chance to touch something utterly unknown, something not of this world—wouldn't you take it?"

I keep my eyes on those far bright trees. "I didn't have a choice."

Like he was struck, "Right."

We stand next to each other for a long time. He keeps opening and closing his mouth. Finally he goes, "I wish you could have seen how beautiful it was."

There's something in his voice I recognize. His hunger chimes with mine. Like maybe if we devoured each other, deep inside the other's gut, we'd both find peace.

He puts a hand on my waist, doesn't flinch when he feels the lumps. He lays two fingers on my face. "You're so beautiful."

I start to shake. "You should get me home." I'm feeling full of fire, I'm feeling untouchable, I'm thinking no, no, he couldn't kiss me any more than he could kiss the hot edge of a knife.

Our lips meet.

One of his hands slides between my legs. We both gasp. He kisses my neck.

"You don't deserve pain," he says to my skin, "you don't deserve any of this. Let me—please?"

There's some sad little part of me that thinks he's offering to undo it all. The rest of me knows this is a stupid weak hope, not God nor Jesus and certainly no scientist has power like that. But still. The huge sweetness of this thought, I lean into it.

He peels off my clothes there by the river. I pull or he pushes us back against a tree. The bark scrapes my back and I shiver like way back on that cold morning in August. My heart is exploding blood through me. Every beat hurls the globes against my skin. He stares at me for a minute and I think he's forgotten how to breathe. Then he pulls me to him, wet kisses down the center of my chest and each rib and my belly. His knees press into the mud.

"So beautiful, so beautiful." His breath tickles my stomach. "I'm so sorry, so sorry."

He kisses the lumps, lips brushing the crest of each dome. His kisses make them churn. "Who ever deserved to see beauty like this?" He lays his cheek against them, nuzzles them with his nose. "I don't deserve it. I don't deserve this."

I stare across the river at the trees though the sun is almost down now, their fire smoldering out. The river under its sluggish skin runs fast and cold. They brought me here when I was little, once, they taught us about the water cycle. The scientist enters me like a plea, like somewhere at my core lies the promise of his own absolution. He seeks it again and again.

What happens the next week is pale blue slips show up tacked to our doors. *Properties in the indicated area have been designated unfit for habitation. Domain is hereby transferred to a redevelopment firm. Current residents have two weeks from notification date to complete relocation.*

I know there was a time when I would have gotten mad about this. When I would have looked around at the apartment—the view through our window and the spot where Dean rollerbladed into the door and the Eiffel Tower picture I taped to the wall—and gone wild at the thought of leaving. But now it's like someone's yelling at me from very far away, almost too far for me to hear, and I just can't see how it could be that important.

"They're tearing down our houses?" Trini says from the couch. Trini doesn't get off the couch anymore. Then she just starts laughing and laughing except her laugh sounds basically like a grunt.

Dean and I start to pack our stuff. At least I think we're packing but I can't tell if we're really getting anything done. I keep putting things in boxes and taking them out and refolding them. Dean finds Mom's clothes crammed onto a high shelf and pulls them all down, fluttering avalanche of rayon and polyester over his head. He presses his face into her dresses, gasps in like he wants to pull the fabric into his lungs.

Out in the street we show each other the blue notices, we ask where are people headed, we shake our heads. One thing that's changed is we touch each other more. Even people I barely know, instead of saying hi we just brush our palms over the hills in each other's skin. We move like people who are sleepwalking, we move like people who are about to wake up.

The only person who doesn't act like they're dreaming is Dean. He stands on the bleachers in Paige Clifton field wearing one of Mom's old nightgowns. The dead-eye kids crowd the grass in front of him, reach up to touch his hem.

He howls, "*We are the mothers of new creation! Do you feel the power growing inside you? Why do you think they want to drive us out?*"

His face is unspeakable. More people pause at the edge of the field, listening.

"*They fear us. They fear our children.*" His voice climbs up to a shriek. "*They may cast us out of here, but we will spread across the country! We will spread across the planet! When it comes it will come to all of us, and it will not be denied, and every place on Earth will know our glory!"*

Everyone listening starts to whoop and sway. A breeze picks up and Mom's nightgown billows around him and fills with light and his bony lumpy body is silhouetted through the white fabric. Really I have no idea anymore, who can even say, he could be my little brother or he could be a goddess born in the center of the sun, come to walk with us through the fire of these last days.

On our final night in the fourplex I go out into the backyard. It really wasn't that long ago that we stood here and whooped for the Magic Factory to get going already. There's no glitter or glow anymore. Only the plain sky, filthy with regular stars. For every one I count, there's one more. For every world that lets you down there's another, and another, promising redemption. It's strange looking up at them. They flicker and pulse and from inside me come answering pulses and I know without knowing that what's inside me is the same as what's up there. I'm flayed down to nothing but a thin boundary of skin between two fields of stars.

You know when I think about my life there's not really a lot I got to choose. Mostly what I did was because we'd be evicted otherwise or because there was a coupon for it and I never spent too much time freaking out about that. But now I have this new feeling like something has loosened I didn't even know was tight. Like the gentlest stream ever is carrying me away. Like I don't have to worry anymore about anything, no regrets or what-ifs, because before I go, I'm going to make something beautiful.

Maybe I'll be the sound, the music that was never music. People all over will hear me and freeze and just start crying where they stand. Or I'll be the stars that gush up into the sky and rain down over the highway. All the cars will come screeching to a halt and everybody will reach out their windows for the lights falling around them and laugh and know that there is love everywhere in the world even where you don't imagine it could survive. Or I'll pour into a spring of clear shining liquid, I'll flood the streets and wash away the sticks and trash and broken glass and you can come out and dip your Dixie cup in and gather me up. One drop on your tongue and your scrapes will heal, your teeth will straighten, your feet will soothe. One sip and your daddy will come home. A cupful and, come close now, no one will ever lie to you again. The world will be set on fire with justice. All the things you hunger for will fly close like tame hummingbirds. Just reach out—*oh God*—just take it.

Moonkids

Suzo says moonkids find their way to Sandpoint because they're drawn to the tides. They like to be around something else that's ruled by the pull of the moon. Colleen thought she came to Sandpoint because Crabby Abby's was hiring and soft shell didn't seem like such a bad thing to eat for lunch every day, but she's willing to concede that maybe Suzo has a point.

At any rate, there are a lot of moonkids in town, which mostly Colleen likes though every so often it makes her crazy. She's been here a year. She likes that Suzo lets her wait tables instead of keeping her kitchen side. Plenty of other restaurants keep moonkids kitchen side on account of the odd asshole customer who makes a snide comment about moonies putting him off his food. Suzo's into jumping on stuff like that. "This is an equal opportunity place of employment," he'll say, "and at this point I'd like to give you equal opportunity to get the fuck out of my dining room."

No denying it, though. Moonkids, they're kind of stubby. On account of them growing up on the moon. Your muscles learn differently in moon gravity. Your bones form light like a bird's. Used to not even be possible to make the transition, you'd touch down into earthpull and collapse like fast-melting candles. Too many fractures for all the king's horses and all the king's men. Way, way too many for Earth doctors to deal with. (Earth doctors are known for not giving a shit.) Now, though, they've got ways around it. They've got operations and stuff. Every moonkid's got incision scars in the same places.

Colleen likes that her friend Tesla works for Suzo too. Tesla got promoted to assistant manager a couple weeks ago, because she's so bomb with the business side of things. Encouragement is good for Tesla. The people side of things, she has more trouble with.

The restaurant is hopping today. Some obscure holiday. Some excuse for moneybags to wallow in a day at the shore. Big wellfed families sit around the tables and snork down crab bisque and get a total kick out of summoning, "Waiter? Oh, waiter!" The air droops with fish smells and the sweaty fervor of overtipping. Everyone likes reliving the golden consumer boom once in a while.

Colleen sloops between tables like a freaking old school rollerskateress. Shrimp poppers here, cod basket there. She can recommend the most expensive thing on the menu in a way that doesn't feel sleazy. She takes orders without a pad. The food is grody but the moneybags pay for service, for the anachronistic privilege of *getting served*, and the tips are spinning out like cotton candy and Colleen's feeling on top of the world.

It's been a year since she last stumbled and spilled someone's calamari. A year since she overthought the business of walking in earthpull and smashed down and had to have two people haul her upright. A year since anyone watched her flailing and tittered and edged away.

Colleen, you'd look at her today and you'd say, now there's a moongirl who's *coping*. Mostly, you'd be right.

Tesla isn't doing as well.

The customer rush today, it means big tips but also big noise, and they've got a sous chef out sick and fifteen other things and all Tesla wants is to get the purchase order in but instead she's smudging the e-paper with her elbows, biting eight of her fingernails at once. Tesla feels people staring even when they're not. She starts to twitch. She picks her lips until they bleed, and then people ogle the chick with blood down her mouth and then she picks more frantically and a feedback loop gears up. Stop, Tesla, sweetheart, hush. Moongirl par excellence. Bones too frail for all the muscle, mind too frail for all the grief.

After work they go down to the boardwalk, horking up salt air to swab the deep-fryer smell out of their nostrils. Tourists are sparse here, their enthusiasm thinned by sparser raindrops. Tesla digs her nails into the sag of Colleen's upper arm, pushes her nose into Colleen's shoulder. Colleen imagines she smells like sweat but doesn't pull away. Earthpull is fickle like a trickster gnome. Sometimes even after months and months it sneaks up behind you and punches in your knees.

A mother with a whole flock of kidlets snotting behind her passes the two of them. Every single head in the flock turns, eyes swell up with the witnessing of something *other*. Mama swats their heads. "They're Lunarian, honey. You keep walking. You know what Lunarians do?"

Colleen appreciates how mom tries to keep her voice low. But she could polish up the explanation. Excuse me, ma'am, we're moonkids, she could say. Don't let real Lunarians catch you mixing us up. Lunarian, fancy word, reserved for the fancy few who claim residence up on the cheeseball. I haven't been Lunarian for three years and seven months. Want to see my certificate of dismissal? Signed by the head of the exam board and the council chairman and the CEO himself (that one's probably a stamp.) With this piece of paper, we divest you of your homeland. Where you were born, it doesn't want you anymore.

As the kidlets trot away Tesla whimpers, and Colleen nips two fingers on the rough of her elbow.

"Fuck em, Tes, you know?" she whispers. "Just keep saying it in your head. Fuck em, fuck em, fuck em."

Moonkids, every now and then, they treat themselves to a little rage.

Tesla and Colleen, bestest friends, didn't meet on Luna. Sat for the exams in the same hall, rode the same bus down to Earth, didn't lay eyes on each other until they were poured onto the asphalt with fifteen other fresh chucked moonkids. Blinking in the alien sunlight, bus seat patterns still printed on their thighs. With their heavy torsos and brittle spiderlimbs. Tesla was tallest, Colleen remembers, arms startlingly long and a look on her face like she was moving pebbles with her mind.

They met. Their skin shivered, sixteen sterile years now swamped with hotness. "How about you?" Colleen spoke first. "What's your plan?"

"Oh. We have the same shirt." Tesla flapped her spider arms. "Awkward."

They all had the same standard-issue shirt, draped over their bodies like towels flung on spilled drinks, but Colleen didn't catch the joke until Tesla had already begun to laugh.

They hiked the beaten-down Maryland countryside, figuring out step by step just how much jack shit ten years of moon education did for you. Tesla can solve fifth-order partial differentials in her head, Colleen can recite a hundred places of pi like a bedtime story, but could either of them get hired as a sales clerk? *You're not really the image we look for in retail.* Variations of that line droned out ad infinitum. Maybe if your legs weren't bowed? If your spine didn't crook? If your body wasn't running down itself like hot wax and your eyes didn't bore straight into the back of my skull?

In so many hack hostels clinging to plugged in towns, they lay on cotton comforters crusted to a shine. They discovered wine and how it improved their impressions of the assholes they'd met that day. "Yo, chicka, tell me," Colleen polished her Earth drawl, "is it really made of cheese?"

"Man or rabbit?" Tesla snorted and smeared the nanopaint she was dabbing on her cheeks. "Man or rabbit, man or rabbit?"

In the latenight Colleen listened to the tiny noises Tesla made in her sleep. Whimpers from a tongue and lips newborn.

They never said anything about heading for the coast. Never talked much about any direction at all until one day they got off a bus and threw their heads back and inhaled weedy brine. Salt-fingered wind started thinning through their hair. A jewelryman on the sandy street clacked his tongue, booted them on their way with pale bruising eyes, but in a few blocks they found the restaurant. Flat-roofed Crabby's, crusted with pre-aged kitsch. Suzo picked a red mole on his neck and looked Colleen up and down. "You can do weekends?"

Girl thought the question was rhetorical, took her three minutes before she remembered to answer, yeah. Yes.

In the gray mornings and clouded nights they put on loose clothes and go down to the beaches. They learn what it's like to regret little things. They track sand through sublet rooms and wake up with tooth-sweaters and crud in their eyes. This thing, Colleen wonders, does it count? As a kind of living? Feels more like yanking free driftwood that waves have buried under sand. But what else would you call it?

Today Trespass joins them on the boardwalk. Trespass is Tesla's younger brother, with the ignoble honor of being the second in a family to flunk off the moon. Trespass is kind of a bamf. He named himself. He shaves the crown of his head and paints his face in bright white segments. He insults people in loud, clinical terms. He carries his moonbulk like bounty from a hunt and swings his fists often enough that no one's fooled by the whisper-squeak of his voice.

And at moonrise? He sits on the sand and sobs like a girl.

He comes up behind them as they lean on the railing and claps a hand on each one's shoulder. "Ladies. How does it shake?"

Colleen laughs and shoves him away but Tesla doesn't move at all. She has her chin on her palm and her elbow propped on the boardwalk railing and she slides her elbow out so that her whole upper body sinks lower. She purses her lips and stares out at the ocean. The moon is out in the sky this afternoon, soft as an exhalation on a cold window. None of them ever look up at the sky but they can all feel it, feel the finger it brushes along the backs of their necks.

Trespass whistles a seagull trill. "Oh, big sister. You still sweating Guy McAdams?"

Guy McAdams is a rrriot shield of an Earthborn dude who slides his body through too small waves with too big flash. Guy McAdams wears a state-of-the-art repelling suit when the water is 72 degrees. But that's perfectly Tesla, who has always liked falling in love with shiny outsides. Her crushes rail like silent storms and then dissipate so fast that Colleen doesn't even argue anymore, just stocks up canned goods and rides them out.

Trespass, though, can't resist a few digs. "Guy McAdams, that dude's a human Pap smear. If Guy McAdams were a sno-cone flavor, he'd be strawberries and shit."

Trespass, if you couldn't tell, is hellbent on milking every last drop out of his teenage years. "Dude, I spent sixteen years in front of a screen," he tells anyone who listens. "Sixteen years, I got force-fed science like one of those foie-gras ducks. And now I'm free? Failing those exams, I swear. Best thing ever happened to me."

What Trespass won't tell you is that his score was zero point six points away from being a passing grade. One corrected formula, one fewer stray pen mark, and he could have made it. Could have gotten the gold confetti and a hand-drawn banner over his pod door—welcome, Scholar of the Lunarian Research Academy! Pillar of our scientific society, jewel of our education system, Mom and Daddy's golden boy. Welcome, welcome!

What Trespass won't tell you is that for the first three weeks after he came down to Earth, he sat on the bathroom floor in Colleen's apartment and shivered. Turned the shower head on, and off, and on.

Tesla's curled up inside her funk and not coming out to play, so Trepass turns to Colleen instead. "Hear there's a new girl turned up? Out of Station 65, I think. I heard she went around to Suzo's looking for work."

Colleen snorts. "A seal could get work with Suzo." She stretches her arms out and pokes Tesla's shoulder.

Two middle-aged women mince past and gawk out of the corners of their eyes. Their lips purse into little bouquets of well-isn't-that-unfortunate. Trespass rounds on them.

"What you looking at, colostomy bags? Yeah I thought so. Get the fuck away."

Here's the deal.

The Earth isn't fit for much anymore. Everyone's given up growth cold turkey, which means they seize on development like an ex-smoker chewing pencils. The moon helps out with that. Luna, her airtight cities full with scuttling hordes of washed out researchers, working like spastic cogs in the breakthrough machine. Hacking away at the mystery forest while they wait for the real trees to grow back.

Except no one's yet figured out a way to get people to work so hard they don't have time to screw. Even mondogeeks get the pole in the hole every now and then. Plenty of those poindexter fetuses end up down the chutes where they belong, but sometimes someone gets a bee in their bonnet about being *parental*, having a *family*. So you end up with moonkids. You can keep your moonkid, superfun pet that it is, until it turns sixteen. Then they give out tests. The ones who pass get fitted into the machine. A nerdlicious parent-and-child cog set, how adorable! The ones who don't—who choke during the multiple choice or blank out during the neural net scan or just maybe admit during the oral exam that there's a part of them that's uncertain, that *wonders*—they're out. The population board picks you up by the scruff of your neck and dropkicks you the two hundred thousand mile ride down to Earth. The moon doesn't give a shit where you go after that. You sucked the moon's tit for sixteen years and had the gall to turn out stupid. The moon never even looks back.

Moonkids are lucky enough to get screwed two ways. Inferior to the Lunarians because of cold hard calculation, and no one knows better than Lunarians that numbers don't lie. Inferior to Earth people because—well just look at them. Limbs so breakable, veins popping out, fat pulling their torsos and thighs. The real Lunarians, when they come to Earth, they get on this high horse of sure I'm ugly but I invented those cosmeds you're sucking down. Your interfaces, your genmodding? Where do you think that comes from, huh?

Moonkids don't even get that. Moonkids get the illustrious task of trucking out slabs of beer-battered cod to shiny tourists who look at them like they're furniture. Yes ma'am, thank you ma'am. Would you like fries with that?

And at night, they get the pain of watching the moon rise.

. . . .

The next morning when Colleen gets to Crabby Abby's, there's the new girl up front getting the tour from Suzo. Wild long hair cascading down her back and apple cheeks that force her eyes into a squint. Her body jiggles, quavers all the time, and Colleen bites her lip in sympathy. She remembers how it was, holding every muscle tense, earthpull like an anvil dropped on your shoulders. When new girl sticks out her blue-veined hand though, Colleen reconsiders. There's a flash in the girl's eyes like spume from a motorboat.

"Ibiza," she introduces herself. "Glad to be here."

Colleen is bemused. New girl's voice is deeper than she expected, raspy. Most moonkids their first year don't speak above a squeak. Ibiza must be screaming to make herself heard. You don't need to do that, Colleen thinks. We get it here. We'll take care of you.

"I'm happy to have a job," Ibiza says. "But I don't want to be taken care of. It's important to blend in, I get that. I'm gonna work hard."

Suzo says, damn straight you are, and leads new girl away before Colleen can figure out if her mind got read. She shakes herself and follows.

New girl is harsh on the customers and harsher on herself when she makes mistakes. Colleen says over and over, it's okay, that's how you learn, and Ibiza snaps, no patronizing. I'll do better. By the end of the night she can recite the whole appetizer menu from memory and when her shift ends she pulls a fistful of tips from her apron (the moneybags think it's a hoot to pay with cash) and kisses the bills. "Check it. I'm rich!"

It's only as the two of them exit into the evening that Colleen realizes Tesla never showed up to work.

. . . .

Ibiza smokes behind the restaurant, cupping her hands around the stickarette. "I can't stay here for long, you know?" Hot brightness in her eyes as she looks at Colleen. "I want to do something. Politics. Law. Back there they never told who was making decisions for us. I want people to listen to me." The certainty in her voice is startling. Politics, law. Colleen tries not to laugh. But come on, who does that junk anymore? The Earth doesn't know law. The Earth knows pleasure, pouring out of the fountain, and as soon as you get close enough to dip your cup you drink down enough to ignore the people who can't get a sip. Politicians are sad gray people, turned on by drudgery. Colleen tries to picture new girl like that.

Ibiza slides her fingers over her forehead and flips her long hair away from her face. Tosses the stickarette away. "Course I got to stop looking like a gob of mud first. This job isn't so bad for that. I'm gonna get rich quick if they keep making me cover shifts for that other moonie. What's her name? Edison? What's wrong with her?"

Colleen knows she should defend Tesla. She bites her lip. She watches the dark strands of Ibiza's hair settle around her shoulders. Forces her eyes to move to the sidewalk, where the stickarette is dying like a star.

"It's a new cycle." Colleen shrugs. "Luna's waxing. Sometimes that—she doesn't feel so good. You know?"

"Waxing. Huh." Ibiza rolls her eyes skyward in consideration. "Never thought of that."

. . . .

Bamp chicka bamp bamp. Party on the beach. Not a cool-party obviously, because it's moonkids, but party nonetheless. Moonkids in bargain bin clothes that curtain their heavy bodies, stick limbs emerging coated in nanopaint, bodysnakes, glowing like so many anemones in the dark night water. On the outskirts a few drunk bodykite dudes whose standards don't go much narrower than "bipedal."

Cool or no, moonkids didn't spend sixteen years getting educated for nothing. They spend their surplus smarts with abandon. They build music machines that wail like electric banshees. They synthesize party pills that sing you up into the clouds.

Colleen weaves through bodies, searching for Tesla. People call out to her, pat her shoulders. Hey, Colly, my girl. How does it go? I owe you one. You owe her one? I owe her *three*. Almost any moonkid who's gotten here in the last three years, they've cried on Colleen's shoulder. They've knocked on her door at midnight and been let in. Colleen halfsmiles, slides out of their grasp. She likes watching people braid together.

Trespass lurches up. His round face painted half white, half black. He pushes a beer into her hand. Cold. Condensation shocks her palm, makes her smile.

"Thanks, T. Seen big sister?"

His nose scrunches and paint flakes onto his shirt. "Not tonight. She's in a dark phase, isn't she?"

Tesla lives her life too raw, thinks Colleen. It makes her easy to love and hard to protect. One time she sat on the beach for two straight days. Let the tide wash in and over her up to her neck, then out again, leaving her seaweed strewn and quaking. Then in. Then out.

Ibiza has been crowned queen of a circle of sand. Boys hold her hands and she swoops and bobs between them. "Fuck this pull," she crows. "I've got an appointment next week. Just wait. I'm gonna get my bones scraped straight. I'm gonna get this bulk shaved off."

Someone hoots. "Ye-ha. Like you got the credit for that."

Ibiza bends an ear to her shoulder so all her hair flows to one side. Her eyes are bladesharp. "I've got ways. Just wait. I'm gonna get jewels set into my kneecaps. I'm gonna get chimes in my ears so when you go bla all I hear is *music*." Girl wrenches herself away from the boys and collars one of the kite dudes. "If this dude"—she jabs his chest—"if this dude can get body-modded for fucking *surfing*, why would I ever sit around looking like an ugly lump? *Fuck* that."

Kite dude looks bewitched. He is touching a moongirl and somehow it's not disgusting. He traces a finger along Ibiza's face and she smirks and snaps her teeth at him. "You know, on Luna, I was four inches taller? Now I'm squashed down." She grabs kite dude's hand and runs it along the lumpy flesh below her armpit. "All this? These are *compressional* folds."

Colleen looks on with weird feelings beating mothwings in her chest. She thinks she should calm Ibiza down. She thinks she should inform her, those body mods? They're for moneybags. Not us. It doesn't do any good calling people ugly. What does good is keeping your head down. Making it from one day to the next.

But she can't make herself step in. Watching a moongirl crow like that, some deep part of her grows honeywarm. It makes her think, maybe all these years she's been aiming at the wrong target. Maybe there are other kinds of hope.

When Ibiza lurches forward and grabs Colleen's shoulders and hollers, "How about you, C? Be a movie star with me!" Colleen grins and blows kisses to pretend paparazzi.

And then someone is yelling. "Here! She's heeeeeere!" All heads turn waterward. It's Tesla, bawling, pointing with both hands. Over the ocean a halfmoon is rising. Laughter simmers down. No one touches the volume but the music fades to a background lub-lub. Oh-oh, hey, Luna. Fancy seeing you here. What a small world.

Colleen walks over and puts an arm around Tesla. "Hey, honey. Shh." Tesla leans so that her tears fall on Colleen's shirt.

One of the kite dudes starts singing "Buffalo Gals" and Colleen hears Trespass growl. "Buffalo, motherfucker? You want buffalo? Buffalo fucking *stampede*."

She turns in time to see Trespass haul out and clock a dude in the face, and then the brawl is on, and of course Trespass will win, though he will end it wheezing and choking on the sand. Ibiza has disappeared. Colleen scans the shore and finally catches a mini figure hiking up into the dunes, long hair trailing behind her, back turned to the moon.

"You must be disgusted with me." Tesla flops her head into Colleen's lap. Girls are on the futon couch in Colleen's apartment. Just one room on the first floor, with an afterthought of a bathroom and a kitchen stowed away in one corner. But her front door slides open on to a sandy street, and across the street is sandy sidewalk, and past that is the roaring sucking spitting old man sea.

Colleen pets Tesla's hair. "I'm not disgusted with you."

"Then you're a saint. I'd be disgusted with me." The room smells like lemons and salt-stiff clothes.

This afternoon Tesla spent locked in the Olde Tyme Quik Mart bathroom. Some brashmouth Earth lady tried to pick her up in the oral hygiene aisle, and fragile girl freaked.

"She called me, lu-mi-nous be-ing." Tesla rolls the words on the front of her tongue for disgusted emphasis. "She said something about devotion. She probably wanted me to go recharge her goddamn crystals."

Colleen does a belly laugh that makes Tesla's head shake up and down. "You should have—you should have done her star charts. Blown her fritzy mind."

Tesla groans and reaches out to play with the rocks on the side table. Colleen likes rocks smooth, symmetrical, ovoid. She brings them home and finds that anyone who comes through the apartment likes to cradle them. Big as a finger, big as a fist. Earth-bones in every color. Tesla lays a gray green pebble in each palm and rubs them with the hams of her thumbs. Holds them up to her ears like secret-listening. Brings them to her lips like a kiss.

Colleen's distracted by a phantom pressure on her upper arms. She worries at the memory until she can place it—Ibiza's hands at the party shaking her shoulders, pulling her close. She twists her head and presses her mouth to her armflesh. Why? Dunno. Seeking a taste. Like how the ocean's touch leaves behind fingerprints of salt.

Suzo has a bunch of people over at his pieced together house. Ibiza shows up with legs like strange long twigs. Bulk still on her belly and ass but her hips all carved away. She walks like a newborn fawn. Cackles like a raven.

"*Told* you. I *told* you I'd do it. Ugly mugs thought I was full of shit, but I told you. Doctor had a big laser, it was over in ten minutes."

They ask how she paid for it and she says, "Fill out the right forms. Smile at the right people. It was state of the fucking art,

I'll tell you that. I'm doing this shit right." She flings her arms out, shakes her hips. "Next stop, torso! Next stop, shoulders! Next stop, face!"

Colleen stays out of the fray though all night she can feel Ibiza raking her with her eyes. Finally Colleen slips out the sliding door and stands on the sidewalk, leaning against the vinyl siding of the apartment building. Tesla's funk is making her anxious. She thinks about how it's like some people have a broken vase inside them. The pieces never quite fit back together.

She turns and finds Ibiza right up in her face.

"Holy shit."

"Sorry." Ibiza looks the opposite of sorry. She nudges Colleen. "Hey. Uh. I wanted to ask you a question. I heard a thing about you."

Oh, yeah. At some point or another everyone hears a thing about Colleen. She tries to look like she doesn't know what Ibiza means and doesn't want to. Like that'll make the girl go away.

"What I heard," Ibiza grinds the gristle of her question, "is that you didn't take the exams."

Yep, that's what they hear. Colleen stands perfectly still and stares out across the parking lot. Then really slow she brings her head up and down.

It's the first time she's seen Ibiza struck silent. Girl doesn't ask why not, but it's in the cant of her head and the tap of her fingers, so finally Colleen answers.

"I didn't want to do research. Didn't want to be a scientist. Had some dumbass idea about art." She laughs at herself, bitter sealbark.

Yeah, Colleen, you thought you were pretty freaking cool, didn't you? Sitting in the exam room with your hundred classmates, typing dirty limericks into the answer screens. Hitting the submit button and sending in fifty-six pages of blank, blank, blank. You were going to stick it to the man, you were going to shuck off your parents and your friends and your whole little sanitized, climate-controlled life, all in the name of that skanky pagan god called art. You lovely fucking revolutionary.

But there were those first months when she arrived on Earth and found it so full of artists its eyes were turning tie-dye. When she tried to enroll in a narrative school and got laughed out of the admissions room. Because the truth is, Colleen, in this post-consumer post-information fever dream of a world, creativity is a vital fluid. The inhabitants of these cities swim in virtual galaxies. They sculpt their bodies into fairytale shapes. They lick the lines between reality and fantasy, body and mind, until everything melts together like ice cream.

All because of Luna. Gleaming white sacrificial lamb. It took three years for Colleen to get this. Research happens on Luna, so pleasure can happen on Earth. The beautiful Earth people, they don't have time to concern themselves with the twitching blinking nerdmen from the moon. They for sure don't have time for some flabby beach bum kids who wobble when they walk.

So Colleen falls back on what she knows. She soothes Tesla and she rolls her eyes at Trespass. She's good at giving people a place to crash. She's good at serving fried food. When she dreams of the moon her visions are colored amethyst and silver and midnight. The desolate gaping plains of home wake her up with tears streaming down her cheeks. She'd like to dig her nails into random people on the street. Moonkids know pain, she'd shriek to them. Moonkids could make beauty. But she doesn't. Oh Colleen, no one wants to hear about that.

Ibiza grabs her wrist. "I knew there was something. Something. You don't go around moping like everyone else." Her fingers palpate up Colleen's forearm. "You're so tense."

Colleen tries to pull away. She wants to say, Tesla doesn't mope, but that's such a lie. And it's true about the rest of them too, how they shiver, how they cling. Sometimes it builds like sludge on her brain until she wants to fling them all into the ocean.

"I told myself I'd be different." Ibiza scrutinizes Colleen's wrist. "I knew I'd fail. I was never any good at that shit. I figured, might as well embrace it."

She doesn't say anything else because Colleen leans in and kisses her.

Somehow they are down the street and in Colleen's apartment and on the futon. Ibiza's hands are up her shirt, tracing orbits around her breasts. The moon is hidden behind clouds tonight, a milky haze that leaches through the window. Colleen reaches for Ibiza's hips and peels her shorts down. The scar from her bone shave runs down the outside of her leg from hip to knee. The skin is sunken and gray. A line of pale pus oozes between the stitches and catches the moonlight.

"It doesn't hurt." Ibiza puts a hand on Colleen's cheek and forces her eyes away from the wound. "Leave it."

Her words rasp in a language Colleen doesn't understand. Her long hair hangs in her face, brushes over her stomach. She must have been growing it for years on Luna, Colleen realizes. She must have *planned* to let it down. The clouds shift and for a moment the moon gets an eyeful of them, then is obscured.

Colleen clamps one of Ibiza's legs between her own knees, shoves her other thigh up with her hand. Leans down, breathing hard, sticks her tongue into the dark. New girl tastes like clam juice. Which is to say salt water, and body. Ibiza makes a noise like a gull. Something shakes in her thigh. Then she sits up and pushes Colleen back. Her eyes are dark and liquid and Colleen thinks she sees something broken open. Ibiza licks her lips.

"You," she says, "you could be Lunarian." Her voice is thick with longing.

Colleen has thought about this every day for three years. She imagines filling in the exam blanks with serious answers. She imagines filling them in with her whole brain and whole heart. She can picture the congratulations, the celebrations, the cool close embrace of her family and the tunnels of Luna.

She shrugs at Ibiza. "No, I couldn't. I've been here long enough to figure that out."

Ibiza shakes her head stubbornly. "But you don't know for sure."

Suddenly the three years that separate them feel like ages. Three years of earthpull, of fighting, of just barely making it. They stretch miles wider than Colleen's whole childhood on Luna. "If I had passed, there are other things I would never have known. I made a choice. I'm not really any different."

And you aren't either, she thinks. *I didn't see that at first.* She reaches out to pet Ibiza's shoulder. The other girl's questions drive sadness into her like a wedge. Her mouth is dry.

Ibiza pulls away. "You are different," she insists. The door that had cracked open in her eyes now so fast clangs shut. "We're different." There it is, back in her eyes, the tinge of distaste that makes her look more like an Earth girl than any body mod ever will. She is retreating and retreating like the tide. They sit in silence for a moment. Then Ibiza stirs. "I think I should go."

She pulls her shorts on, inhaling as the fabric skates over her scars. Colleen doesn't turn and watch her go out the door.

. . . .

So. Sandpoint. Crappy little gum wrapper town. Undeserving of so many stories. So much love. But this not quite ground and not quite water, they own it. This sliver of country with its everchanging dunes and sinuous shoreline, it's theirs. Knowing is a kind of possession, and they know where the tidepools form, where the weed is sold, which beachfront property owners don't mind if you cut through their yards. Inconstant, of course, but remember they're moonkids. They're used to not owning things for real.

They were raised in homepods doled out by the government. The moon knows sleeping space and study space. The moon knows regulated recreation zones and one vacation day per month. The moon knows you are part of the machine, and it presses that knowledge in on you, it gives you disposable clothes and flavorless food and raises you with the knowledge that you too are only worth the research you produce, sweet little cogs of mine.

Funny, then, sick and sad, how souls find something to latch on to even in the bleakest environs. How hungry bodies are to belong. Little Lunarian kids, their brains know nothing is guaranteed, but their hearts cling like hermit crabs on driftwood as the tide comes in. December after they turn sixteen, the exams come. The wind whips up the water. January, the scores get mailed out. CRASH. Big waves slam down, froth and churn, and when the water recedes again, some of those crabs, those cogs, those bright-eyed girls and boys are swept clean away.

. . . .

In the night Colleen flees down to the beach, kneels by the water. Sand collapsing all swirly around her legs. She puts her mouth into the sea and inhales and the salt water barrels down her throat like a bullet train. Burns tracks into her tongue. Girl falls backward, coughing. Her hair goes smack in the wet sand.

Turn her head one way, down the beach there is an old petrol car parked on the sand, people dancing like paper cutouts in the headlight glow. They kick up shells and gallop down to the wateredge to scream and spit. Turn her head the other way, up the beach is a dark slick shape of something. Big jelly or rotten tire or selkie skin. Salt and body, the ocean is nothing but salt and body. Colleen drinks sea water til her eyes ache, thinking with each suck, go ahead, put the flame to us. Just see if we melt and flow away. Gulps until her stomach revolts and then she pukes it up and walks the long way into town. By the time she reaches her apartment the sand has dried on her. She brushes it off like dust and climbs into bed sweet and clean.

On the phone with her mother in the pink hour between lunch and dinner rushes. Colleen leans against the sliding glass door and jams the minidisk to her ear. The connection is finicky, it balks and shuffles its hooves.

"Do you"—her mother's voice flickers in and out—"a job?"

Her concern seeps down the phone line. No other question a moon mom could ask, really. No other way to tell: Are you okay? Are you functioning? Lucky Colleen lives in a pleasure park town where things like jobs still exist. Or else how would she explain to the mama, jobs mean goose egg here. We've moved on.

"I'm a waitress, Mom." Like I tell you every time. "I bring people food."

That faint noise might be her mother ohhing or might be the sound of two hundred thousand miles. Colleen waits for more news without expecting any. Machines don't rearrange their parts too often.

"Oh!" Her mother's thin exclamation. "The Sacaros!" Mr. and Mrs. Sacaro live in a neighboring pod. "They're having a baby."

Sharp pain as big chunks of Colleen's chest erode into her stomach, until she takes a quick tight breath. Why does this news smart so bad? Why does she wrench open the door and fling the minidisk into the flowerbed?

Later she'll apologize to the moon mom, explain how the connection fritzed out. And she'll think of how Lunarians see her today. Wonder, if she saw Ma and Pa again, would things be different. Probably no, course not, how could you—but, maybe. Maybe there'd be a little hitch-pause between the moment of recognition and the moment of hugging. Maybe that hitch would grow wider.

It would be easy to call the dark breathless void between them *space*, but Colleen knows it's way older than that, and still no one's built a rocket that can cross it.

One evening Colleen runs into Ibiza on the boardwalk. Not like she's been avoiding her or anything. Not exactly. When she thinks of Ibiza there's an odd sensation in her stomach. Not embarrassment. That she's sure of. More like disappointment. A little like grief. You talked so big, new girl, she wants to say.

I thought you had answers. I though you could fix us like that hack doctor straightened your legs.

They stare at each other. Ibiza licks her lips. Colleen makes a motion with one hand and then stops, not sure where she's going. She shifts her eyes to the people passing them, ogling them in the neardark.

Then she hears her name getting yelled. "Colleeeeeeen!"

Trespass, white faced under his white paint, hurtling up the beach like a cannonball. "Colleen! It's big sister. Get her. Gotta help me get her."

The two of them rush across the beach. No, not two of them. Three. Ibiza runs too. Colleen can feel her joints grind, her muscles fray. Times like this she hates her body the most. This earthpull, this aching flesh. How light we were on the moon. How we could have bounded over miles.

Tesla is walking into the ocean. The water is up to her neck. Waves rear up and come down over her head and she doesn't flinch, doesn't duck, just keeps heading out. It's almost too dark to see her.

Moongirl, come back! They scream through the seabreeze. Hurl themselves into the ocean. At first the water is something to fight, but then it gets deep enough that they can give themselves over to it. They paddle to Tesla, surround her, tug on her arms and kiss her cheeks. Big sister. Best friend. Why would you leave us? The fuck you thinking?

That first moment when they catch her, Tesla's eyes are dead. But she sparks under their touch and her mouth makes a smile.

"I'm okay." Her lips shape the words but her voice is barely a sound. "I'm. I'm okay." Her eyes snag on something beyond all of them.

Colleen and Trespass and Ibiza, they turn and follow her gaze.

A full moon is rising. It catches them off guard. In the ocean they fall silent, still.

Look at them now, only their heads bobbing above the water, four dark bumps breaking up the white shine of the moon reflection. Cradled by the warm ocean, they don't have to be moonkids. They could be round and embracing as Luna herself. They could be slender as the breeze that licks the sea surface. They could be regular Earth boys and girls, loving the feel of water on skin. They could be sea nymphs. They could be four seals.

Ibiza's face is hard and set. She stares at the moon like a challenge. Trespass is quiet, his arms winging back and forth just under the surface. Paint runs down his face and makes a pool of smoke around his throat. Tesla lets out one gasping sob and chokes on sea water. Colleen reaches through the black water and finds her hand. They clutch each other in the darkness.

Colleen leans her head back so water creeps cool onto her scalp. Around her and beneath her, the ocean pushes with hands like continents. Push, drag.

With her head tilted, her vision is filled up with moon. White and brilliant and huge as the sound of blood in her brain. Huge as the pull of home. Can she see the cities on the surface? The pale tunnels that hash through the face of Luna? Can she see her parents sitting down to dinner, bloodshot, sunstarved, their fingers still tapping out equations? Could she notice the extra place setting at the table, the one they look at but never touch?

Oh come on now. Girl doesn't see any of that. Doesn't even imagine it. This time of night, with water lapping at her cranium, the moon is no longer a place. The moon just *is*, bigger than everything, her light flowing out and lifting them up until they are no longer even floating, their bodies have vanished, they are nothing but light.

If we cried out loud enough, Colleen thinks, maybe the moon would turn her eyes back down to us. If we beat ourselves against the Earth, if we let our bones break and our flesh split, maybe that would jar her memory. Her exiled children. Maybe she would fall in love with us again. It is not enough, this warm dry dust, these rocking waters. We will not last very long. Luna? Please? Hold us. Let us go. Let the squalls in our minds grow quiet. Let our bodies gentle. Let all the knots untie.

If You Could Be God of Anything

Can't remember if I was nine or ten when the sex robot fell from the sky. Just after my sister ditched, when mom was twenty-four-seven plugged into her chair, plugged out of her grief. The only ones left to watch me were my brothers Floro and Bello, scarred princes of the scrounge and salvage, which pretty much meant I was left to watch myself.

We were cul-de-sac kids, born in the burbs, sprawled into the sprawl. We lived in the master bedroom of a house so identical to every other house it didn't matter what it looked like. Two-story foyer with water ripple-rotting down the walls. Burns on the ceiling. Flagstone façade that dropped off in chunks and beaned you. The burbs had been spiraling down for sixty years. Hiding holes for sea-rise refugees and space rejects. Shame-shaded wastelands ringing the city pretties. Our lawns were neat because the grass was all dust. Our streets were clean because there was nothing to throw away. City-dwellers flew overhead in their decked out cars, looking down even less often than we looked up.

My brothers had not been home for a week and I spent every morning waiting on the front step, imagining each head that rounded the bend to be one of theirs. That day I was hunkered against the heat, scarfing a pseudosnacker, pink flavor, licking spilled frosting off my shirt. The burbs in summer are the cracked eggshell colors of the houses, the flat dog-belly tan of the dust, the worn-out grey of asphalt and sky. The streets smell like carpet glue.

Dark shapes came round the bend and my heart leapt. Til I realized there were not two but three of them. And how short they were. And that they were Corry, and Leave Alone, and Scram Pha. Skinny boys with scabby elbows, chests concave (though so was my own), mistrusting eyes dark and long-lashed. *Never judge a burb boy by his eyelashes, babydaughter,* my mother told me. *I did, and look what I got.*

The three plowed up the street, Corry trying to keep up with Leave Alone, Scram a cool step behind. Leave Alone would have barreled right past my house but Scram hopped up on my curb.

"Hailo, we saw it fall. Saw a body." He flung a pointing finger toward the west end of the neighborhood, where a century earlier the man had run out of money to build houses on spec and so just quit. Now half-framed colonials speared out of the ground, weathered whale skeletons. They would have been declared hazardous if anyone had felt like making declarations. Instead they became our playground.

"We think s'in one of the houses and we're a find it."

Things fell from cars all the time. Tumbled down from the skyways, burst through the flat clouds. Crumpled-up computers and blipping baby toys and food wrappers that shrieked as they fell. The trash we shrugged off like weather. The treasures we crowed over like manna from citygods.

"You'na come?" Scram cocked his head so far one jug ear touched his bony shoulder.

I had never seen a body. I couldn't have imagined, back then, what it meant to fall. I jumped up, snagged for just a moment on the thought of my still-absent brothers, and ran after the boys. Down one curving street and then another, across cracked-up, bleached-out lawns. Past houses and houses, identical fat white houses, torn-up walks and sagging vinyl and garages with the roofs kicked in because time wore heavy boots. After three streets we were wheezing and the houses were slack-jawed and vacant. This one without windows, this one without a roof. Then no siding, then no Sheetrock.

Then only bones. The bare frames of squat McMansions, their two-by-fours gray and wormy, their foundations crumbling. Something obscene about them, half-birthed but decrepit. Like fetuses left to yellow in jars. The walls were ghostly, permeable, revealing everything. Pipes and wires speared up at strange angles.

We clambered through one and then another, scanning the ground, swinging on the framing. It gave me a nervous thrill to twine in and out of the splintery pine beams, like I was tracking dirt through the soft vessels of someone else's dream. The houses, the neighborhood, everywhere I had ever been my whole life squirmed at my footfalls, breathed out, *we do not want you.*

And we asked, *So?*

. . . .

I was the one who found it. The body. Crumpled between cracked valves from which copper piping had been looted. One glimpse and all the motion went out of me. Because it wasn't a body. Not quite. I opened my mouth to call to the others and found my voice fled. I wanted to turn away, bury it deep—but Scram came up behind me.

"Ossht!"

Which made the other two hop over. *Oh! Woh-woh!*

None of us, then, knew really what it meant to fall.

Amid the rusty pipes in the unfinished bathroom of the half-built house, we squatted and stared at the robot's broken form. Naked except for what must have been a gauzy robe, jewel-bright turquoise, now shredded and bunched around her neck. Her skin luminous brown like it was lit from within, like she would be hot to the touch. It was a glow that people lose when they die, but this thing kept it even now, even shattered.

She looked so human my breath caught in my throat. Something made me think of when my mother shooed us from the room and filled the enamel tub. I never left all the way, peeked through the cracked door, watched her tilt her head back, eyes closed, sluice water over her bare breasts. Mom never looked so happy as when I was gone.

This body, she didn't look happy. Her white eyes were way open and bugged out like some restraint had snapped inside her skull. Her blonde hair much lighter than her skin, snarled by the wind into a single mat that puddled on the concrete. Her wrists and elbows bent the wrong way. One of her legs must have hit the framing as she came down because a beam overhead was splintered and her left shin was missing. Her knee ended in a raw haze of wires, plastic-coated viscera that looked gray until you got close and realized they were every color. Scram got up and ran through one of the unfinished walls, came back holding the shin. "This is a very serious matter." He shook the foot at us like a gavel. "I want you all to do what I say." He shoved the foot right up in my face. Its toenails were painted, hot pink.

He broke the spell and we all quit genuflecting, crowded up around the body. Her torso was punctured by two lines of pale dots, which were, I leaned in and realized, the nub ends of her pseudoribs, driven through her skin by the impact. Corry and Leave Alone crouched together, giggling over her chest. Her breasts lay long and blobby like something inside them had burst and was seeping away. Her nipples large and dark, spooned strangely over jellied flesh. Corry reached out a single finger to press her tit like a button then snapped his hand back. Leave Alone fell over laughing.

I moved to one of her flung-out arms and realized she was missing a hand as well as a foot. This one wasn't ripped but smoothly severed, the edge dark and puckered like someone had sliced through it with hot wire. Unthinking I reached out to stroke her wrist and recoiled. How utterly like skin it was—supple softness with strength underneath. Yet I could see her severed wrist, the mass of wires, no bone no muscle no blood. I reached out again and managed to clasp her wrist, and the realness made my eyes grow hot.

"Hailo, cmere." Scram crouched at her foot. "Cmere lookit this."

I dropped the wrist and walked to him. Scram was two years older than me and I liked it when we got close enough so his arm might brush mine by accident. I knelt and he pointed, "Look."

Between the robot's legs there was nothing. No vagina or skin or hair, just a wide square hole. Her illusion of humanity ended in a gaping plastic port that extended up inside her into darkness. Something in my brain clenched. My stomach roiled. Later my brothers would teach me that those kinds of robots are left empty there so you can plug in whatever apparatus you want, but at that moment a blank terror was blotting out my brain. I was shrinking, the night was encroaching. I squeaked and Scram grabbed my knee. "*Shh*."

No idea why we had to be quiet but I shushed. And thrilled at his hand on my leg. And we crouched together and stared into terrible shadows.

"Oh man." Leave Alone nudged her with his toe. "We should take her back to our fort."

Corry snorted. "How we gonna move her, dummy? She's not walking anywhere."

"We could carry her." That was Scram, standing up. "I bet. If we all helped."

We stared at the body for a moment. "Yeah," I said. "Yeah. Snot like we can leave her here." Which was true though no one knew why.

"Cmon," Scram tugged one of her arms. "Help me."

We joined him. Terrible to feel her loose weight move under my palms. Her body bent in too many places, a bag filled with broken pieces. Eventually we hoisted her onto Scram's back, Corry and Leave Alone bracing her on either side. Her leg dragged on the ground. Her head lolled on Scram's shoulder. Her breasts smushed into Scram's back. I wanted to cry.

We started out of the house, tiny steps, wobbling. Her robe fluttered behind her, gleaming turquoise amid the dust and concrete. "We should get her some clothes," Scram announced. "She can be our queen."

. . . .

The fort was away from the whale skeletons, away from the homes, in a gully where the power lines used to run. Against two real trees we had piled up branches and boards and the door off a wheelie car. It had started out as a place to hide the things we stole. Crinkle packs of food and broken tech bits. One time Leave Alone made off with a whole case of gel candy from someone's front room store. We gorged ourselves for three days until we all shit glowing green. There wasn't much that made it to the burbs that was worth stealing. Sometimes we nabbed photographs, old music players, dug up the only tomato plant in the yard, somebody miss it, please, someone. Miserly place, wouldn't even let us be criminals.

The robot we dumped outside the fort. Scram groaned as her weight eased off him. Propped her up against a real tree and straightened the shreds of nightgown around her body. I tried to close her eyes but her eyeballs bulged like balloons when I pushed the lids down so I left her to gawk.

She gawked as we dragged a dirty skirt out from the fort and covered her legs. She gawked as we draped tattered plastic around her like a smock. She gawked as I twisted her a crown out of TV cable.

Scram and Leave Alone went off to search for rocks. We were going to build a second room for the fort. Corry and I stayed to dig a circle in the dirt. I scraped the ground with a piece of window frame. Beads of sweat crawled down my arms. As I dug I stared at the robot's leg. Her skin was butter smooth and dry.

"Yeah." Corry rocked back on his heels. "I think she's beautiful."

I stared at him. "Shut up."

"What? I do."

I couldn't think of what to say to this. "Huh. You would."

"What's that mean?"

"Nothing. Don't talk to me."

"What?"

But his mind was on the robot, I could feel it, on the little band of belly flesh that showed every time the breeze lifted her smock.

As we worked the boys looked for excuses to touch her. Corry kept brushing his arm along her ankle as he dug. When Leave Alone came back lugging a hunk of cinder block, he heaved it down and staggered, catching his balance by grabbing her neck. Scram kept adjusting her crown, her shawl, brushing his fingertips over her collarbone. Their sweat rubbed off on her, left smudges bright on her poreless skin.

In the distance the deep-down hum of scooters, and my ears perked. My brothers, maybe, on some late-night errand that had dragged into morning. I didn't understand what my brothers did then but I knew it was important. I knew bad things would happen if they messed up. I knew they stayed awake when everyone else grown-up was plugged into games.

About once a month Bello blitzed out on too many tabs, forgot his rule about not letting me on his scooter, pulled me onto his lap and roared onto the highway. *Vroom*. He talked as we sped. "You scared yet, Hai-girl?" His spit flecked my neck before the wind whipped it away. "You gotta get scared sometime." *Vroom*. "How about now?"

He steered with one arm, the other around my waist, the scooter careening crazily across the empty road. My front was numb in the wind but my back against him was warm. His fingers dug so hard into my side that the next morning there would be four parallel bruises. Warehouses and empty lots flew by. *Vroom.* I bit the noises back so hard I tasted blood. "How—about—*now?*"

Eventually he veered around and dumped me on the outskirts of the neighborhood. If I closed my eyes I could still see him speeding away, dark dot on the static country of my eyelids.

I mounded the dug-up earth. Scram and Corry slung down big chunks of cinder block, pried like molars from the McMansion foundations. Every so often I pressed my mouth to my arm, tasted sweat. Feeling my muscles move, it made me happy in a way I couldn't name.

Sometimes when Mom was plugged in I would touch her. Drape her arm over my shoulders, lay my head on her knee. It made me nervous and safe at the same time, to feel her body without her. Here was weight, here was warmth that couldn't leave me, even when all the rest could.

When our stomachs' knuckling could no longer be ignored, Scram dove into the old fort and pulled a phakecake from under a board. It was squished flat but the metallic icing still shone. Divided into quarters, one for each. Scram got the back wrapper, I got the front. Leave Alone and Corry split the cardboard tray, licked it until the paper sogged.

As we ate we asked the robot questions. We had a big metal ball bearing from the construction site and we set it on her sternum. If it rolled off her left side that was yes. If it rolled off her right that was no.

"You have to be very polite," Scram told us like he'd been doing this for years. "You have to say, O Queen, first."

"O Queen, will I marry someone rich?"

No.

"O Queen, will I ride in a skycar some day?"

Yes.

"O Queen, will my uncle who lives in the basement die a horrible death that makes his dick shrivel up and fall off?"

No.

"O Queen, will there be plastipatties for dinner?"

No.

"Yeah that's a big lie." Leave Alone stood up and prodded the robot's thigh. "She's tilted to the right. It's always gonna fall this way. This is stupid."

He went back to piling rocks. I stayed by the robot and asked her more questions in my head.

Are my brothers okay?

No.

Will I ever get out of here?

No.

I picked up the ball bearing and hurled it at her throat, hit her so hard that her head bounced and flopped to the other side.

Again, the dog-growl of scooters, whistles and hacking laughter. "Kid-kid-kiddos! Lookit! That's a big doll you got there, little boys. Sure you can handle it?"

Almost I spun around to say I wasn't a boy but my thumping heart kept me staring at the dirt. "Whatever," Scram mumbled, tearing up a real leaf with his nails. The scooterjocks revved and skimmed away but two whiny trails remained, wound closer to us. They cut out right by our fort and I finally looked up. Against the white sky, a squat gnarled silhouette and a lean restless one. I knew those shapes. Floro, Bello. They were back.

More than double my age. Both short though Bello was just barely taller. So different except they were always together and even now I can't picture them apart.

Bello stood thumbs-in-waistband, bouncing on the balls of his feet. So tense, secondbrother, like the clothespin holding space and time together. Like if he relaxed for a second reality would come flying apart. Floro didn't bounce. Floro was poured out of concrete. Thick bull neck and prettyboy face. He lunged forward and grabbed me around the waist, flipped me upside down so my feet stuck up over his shoulder. "What you looking at, babysister? What, huh? Think we brought you presents?"

The world swung wildly. I could feel the sugar roll sliding back up my gullet. I clenched my teeth. Firstbrother smelled like grease and sweat and something strange, a cloying darkness that clung to my nostrils. "What? What?" Then he caught sight of the robot. "What do you know. Hailo's finally playing with dolls."

He dropped me. I stayed facedown for a moment, breathing in the warmth of the dirt. Waited til my ears didn't ring. When I looked up Bello was right over me, bouncing, bouncing. His face was blank but he thrust out a hand to pull me up. I ignored it.

"You shouldn't of left me."

Bello's eyes narrowed a shade. He wrapped his arms around his torso like maybe it would still his body but he kept bouncing. Silence, and then he nodded. "Yeah. I know."

I stood up. I charged at him and rammed my head into his gut. Bello took it noiselessly, held me at arms' length. "Hailo. Hey. We're here now. We're back."

"What-ever. I'm not stupid, you won't stay." I twisted out of his hands. "You know you won't."

Bello took a deep breath. Chewed his lower lip. His eyes like embers burning up the things he couldn't say. Apologies for what they had done to me. Forgiveness for what I would one day do to them. All he said was, "Probably not."

"Hey bro, come check this out. This worth anything?" Floro beckoned, bent over the robot.

"Not for sale," Scram blurted.

I scuffed a pebble at him. "Shut *up*." It bothered me when other people weren't afraid of my brothers.

Bello shook his head as he walked over. "Nah, they're dropping all over the place. Cheap partydolls. Somebodies up there must be breaking some rules."

We watched my brothers skate their hands over the robot. Scrunch up her shirt and prod her belly. Yank her hair and stare at the back of her neck. My scalp prickled. Bello lifted her severed wrist and flapped it at Floro. "See? They cut out the memory."

"Huh, ladybot." Floro sucked in his breath. "You been through hell."

Then Bello knelt in front of her, tugged off the balloon skirt, and plunged his hand into the hole between her legs. His arm disappeared up to the elbow. His eyes got the blank look of someone concentrating hard on something he couldn't see.

"Ha, ha," Scram said weakly. I didn't want to be watching but I couldn't look away.

Floro squatted near the robot's head, fingers rapping a manic beat on the flesh of her neck. Her head trembled.

It must've only taken a minute but time felt like it was being shredded like Scram's real leaf. Bello withdrew his arm. Shrugged and scratched his scalp. "Everything's fried. Told you. Let's go."

They walked back to their scooters. Floro collared me as he went by, scrubbed his hand through my hair. "Come party with us tonight, babysister? We are taking it eas-*ay* tonight, you bet."

Through the crook of his arm I saw Bello staring hard. He was either examining my bone marrow or he was a thousand miles away. Then he twitched and shook his head like he was unsettling flies. "We'll be around for a while, kay Hailo? Maybe get you some new clothes."

I wanted to press up against them. I wanted us to lie together in our pajamas while I traced my fingers over their scars. I wanted them to try and scare me. One more time. Go on, just try. But they kicked on their scooters and whined away toward the neighborhood.

In their wake we sat around picking scabs, drawing lines in the dirt. I didn't want to look at anyone. The robot was gummy with dirt and other people's sweat. In the distance a bus swooped down bearing tired bodies home from the recycling plant. Through the quiet there came a tiny raspy noise. Corry twitched, "What was that?"

We strained but heard only the vanishing hum of the bus. The sun was backing down. The house frames combed long blue shadows through the dirt. Scram stretched arms over his head. "Probly my stomach. I'm going home."

I didn't move. Home sat in my mind like a hungry hairless animal. I fed it only when I had to. Just when I'd made up my mind to stand, *there*, again the noise, as though it were right by my ear. Leave Alone whooped, "It was her!"

He pointed at the robot.

The four of us froze and watched her. She was utterly motionless. Her head drooped. Her eyes bulged. The shadows of the real trees lay across her sunken belly. We stared until my neck pinched.

"Don't be an idiot," Scram said, kicked dirt at the robot and hiked off toward the neighborhood. The other two followed him, poking each other, shooting scared grins over their shoulders. I stood but couldn't make myself leave. I decided to stamp the floor of the fort down flat. I swept out the real dry leaves that had fallen. There was a leaf on the robot's chest. I flicked it off and my fingernail grazed her breast. Touching her curled my stomach so I forced myself to grab hold of her shoulders with both hands. I leaned down and rested my forehead against her forehead.

"What do you know?" I whispered to her. "You're *trash*. You're not going *anywhere*."

The robot brought her handless arm up to pet my shoulder and murmured, "You smell so good."

I would have screamed if I'd been a screaming-type girl—instead I just fell backward, gasping, my skin lit with fear. The robot's arm fell down limp again but her face twitched. Her distended eyeballs rolled. Her lips flapped like they were trying to escape her face. Her shoulders twisted and the cloth we had draped over her fell away.

"Oh dear!" she giggled. "I seem to have lost my shirt!"

Her voice came from her head but not through her mouth. Full of all the sweet things I had never eaten. Her legs knocked against each other. I realized she was trying to cross her ankles. "I have been bad, haven't I?" Her feet snaked back and forth. "You might have to punish me."

Red waves were breaking over my brain. The world had narrowed to a dark alley with her lipstick prints on the walls but I could see light at the far end and I throttled toward it. Reaching back I groped for the cinder blocks the boys had uprooted. My fingers clutched at one as big as my head. I cradled it in both arms and stood, took a step toward the robot. The wires in her severed arm flexed and fluttered. I hoisted the ancient cornerstone over my head. My biceps screamed. "My!" Her eyes lighted on everyplace but me. "How strong you are!" And I slammed the block down on her face.

Her head collapsed inward. I threw my weight onto the block, crushing the circuitry of her brain. Like crushing honeycombs. I backed off and let the block roll away. Nose split. Lips all over her face. I squirmed my body under the block and heaved it up and again brought it down on her head. Her skin broke into rubbery fragments. Her eyeballs popped and dissolved. Her head a misshapen mass of pale plastic and wire. I ground the paste of her skull into the bark of the real tree.

Then I took the block again and smashed her sternum. I smashed her breasts into the dirt. I smashed her severed wrist until you couldn't guess where arm ended and earth began. I smashed her pelvis and her kneecaps, grated away the fake softness of her skin until she was only a pile of parts, shattered wafers of circuitry and pulverized filaments. I smashed until my muscles wept, until I couldn't inhale without shrieking. Then I collapsed on the mound of remnants, curled around the block, spat out a mouthful of slime. There was no blood. Course there was no blood.

It was dark. The sky was starless but car lights zipped overhead. I stood up all shivery, turned and ran home. If you saw me then you might've thought I had no idea where I was going, but I knew with each step my foot was headed for the ground.

Up the curving staircase with the rotting boards, our room door was open. My brothers sat on the floor, winding the clockwork of their crazy. I stopped in the doorway to watch them, my heart thudding in my throat. Floro hugged his knees to his chest. Bello leaned against the wall, legs splayed out. Tabs trashed about them like fallen petals.

"—nothing left." Floro spat out the words. "And what about us, think we're still pink slick? Think we still ooze when they squeeze?

Bello rubbed a hand over his face. "Nah. We're not dolls."

Floro sprang up. "Want to find out?" He leapt to the other side of the room and came back holding a knife.

Their eyes were glassy. A tendon flexed in Bello's foot. Floro knelt and laid the blade against Bello's lip like a steel mustache. "How about I slice your lips off?"

Bello grinned against the knife edge. "You are such a clown."

"You think? You think I'm joking?

"You're always joking. Ha ha ha."

"Funny, yeah sure. Here's a good one. Fill a body with plastic, what do you think happens? Huh? We're the punch line, littlebrother."

"Okay," Bello shrugged, "for real you want to find out? Here." He thrust his fist out between them. "Cut off my hand."

I stepped into the room. They didn't turn to me but Floro waggled the knife hello. "There's a patty on the windowsill for you, Hai," Bello called. With his other hand he reached out and pulled Floro's knife to rest on his wrist. "I'll show you. Cut off my hand."

I curled up in the window to eat, the frame digging into my tailbone. The yards outside were going shut-eye dark. I sent the fibrous lumps of patty efficiently into my stomach. Food has always seemed like the least pleasurable thing you can still yearn for. In the dark corner Mom was in her chair, plugged in. I didn't look at her. I watched my brothers across the room. They crouched together, staring at Bello's wrist like angels would pour out of it. Floro's hand trembled. Silence clogged everything.

Floro did a dismissive *psh*. "You're a plastic person, little-brother. Like the dolls, like the rest of us."

"Not yet. You'll see. You coward. It'll bleed." Enough hope in Bello's voice to break a window. "I know there's some left."

Oh, my brothers. The ones who taught me not to be afraid of hate. In the dim room they glowed blinding like green balls of fire. Bathed in this light of theirs I could feel a new kind of love. The kind that gives you X-ray vision, that lets you see into the future. If they didn't slit each other open they would die protecting me.

Floro's hand trembled again and Bello snapped, "*Do it.*" If he were a fuse he would be lit, if he were a particle cannon he would be firing. "I'll *strangle you* if you don't."

"Yeah? You'll strangle me if I *do*."

"How'd I strangle you with one hand?"

"Ha!"

"Ha!"

They laughed like they were heaving cinder blocks at each other. The knife pressed a shallow valley in Bello's skin.

The green fire lit them up, showed me what they would find. Sparks and wires, filaments and honeycombs. Inside Floro too—I could see the petal-thin cogs of his brain. The tik-tok mice running, running, turning the wheel of his lungs.

The pressure would burst my eardrums. There was too much of this, always the same thing. I got up and brushed by them on my way out, left them frozen, straining against, against.

I settled cross-legged on our stoop and rested my chin on my hands. In the darkening even the burbs look pretty, the way a shipwreck is beautiful at the bottom of the ocean. The houses swim black-black out of the blue-black night. If I raised my eyes I could catch the blinking of cars flying overhead. Red-white, red-white, though a star-spangled sky. I watched for a moment and then turned my eyes back to the houses. My arms ached from lifting the block. I wrapped them around my skinny chest and felt something warm pulse through me. Not happiness. More like satisfaction. Funny how dropping something heavy can feel just like clutching something close. We in the burbs—we didn't need any kind of robot. We had all been pushed out the car door. We fell the thousand feet, we hit the ground, we got up and kept going.

TEACHER

WHAT WE WERE DOING THAT week was subject-verb agreement. I showed the students pictures of Grayson and Hayley picking strawberries or flying a kite. "If Grayson were talking, would he say, 'I flies the kite' or 'I fly the kite'?"

Thompson raised his hand. "Ms. X, Ms. X, I got a question! What's the red things?"

"Duh, strawberries, idiot," said Alisha. Thompson said he ain't talking to her, big tits. Alisha stabbed a pencil into the back of his hand.

"Ms. X, Ms. X, Ms. X!"

"Yes Nacai?"

"Uh, like, is there a drug, like, it keeps you acting like you're on the drug, even when you're not on it no more?"

"That sounds like PCP, Nacai. Now, if Grayson were talking to Hayley, would he say, 'You pick the strawberries' or 'You picks the strawberries'?"

"I think that's what my dad's on," Nacai said.

In the pictures Grayson and Hayley were always colored with brown skin, for cultural sensitivity.

The curriculum master plan indicated that it was time to distribute the mid-unit assessment, so I did. Devin put his head on his desk and moaned like an old bear.

"Devin, I need you to fill out this assessment so I can know if you're making adequate progress."

"My tooth hurt," he said, and moaned again.

"That's third person, Devin. What ending do you put on the verb?"

"My tooth hurt cause I don't go to the dentist. Cause my mom don't sign up for benefits with the clinic. Cause the clinic open hours when she has to drop my baby sister off at Kiddie Kollege, and she goes once with my baby sister, and they say they don't let you bring children in the benefits office, so we don't go back."

When they turned in their assessments they got a hug from Ashton, our Innovation and Evaluation Intern. Ashton had a spreadsheet, and he recorded each child's name and the duration and intensity of the hug. The goal was to quantitatively determine whether hugs were a worthwhile motivational strategy. Nacai handed in his assessment with only one question bubbled in, and grabbed Ashton around the waist. "Five . . . six . . . ," counted Ashton. "As a college student, Nacai, buddy, I gotta ask you to let go."

Part of Ashton's internship contract stipulated that he begin all of his sentences with 'As a college student . . .'

Nacai didn't let go. Ashton peeled his arms away. "As a college student, I can tell you, the scale doesn't go past six. Nacai. The scale stops at six."

Next week we would start verb tenses, which they sorely needed.

It was time for my performance review with the Vice Principal. "Your assessment results were lackluster," he said.

"It's been seven months since I liked myself," I told him. "I don't think I know how to tell the truth anymore."

"What you need to do," he said, "is create an environment more conducive to learning."

"Sometimes when I speak, I can't hear the words. All I hear is the sound of worms pushing up through wet earth."

The Vice Principal frowned. "There is nothing in our standards-based approach that covers the sound of worms." He leaned forward in his plastic chair. "Let me give you some advice. If I were you, I would maximize instructional time, and minimize misbehavior."

He waited until I had written this down; then he stood up and shut the door. On the back of the door was a poster that said, IF YOU BELIEVE, YOU CAN ACHIEVE. "That curriculum cost us a lot of money," he said. He was close enough that I could feel his breath on my face. "We should discuss how you can provide us with adequate returns on our investment."

. . . .

When I got back to the classroom I found the substitute sitting at my desk making origami boxes. The class had dog-piled Ashton. They were pulling his hair and jumping on his stomach and lying down on him. "As a college student," he gasped out, "I am really not okay with this!"

"He said he was gonna leave us," Alisha told me. "He said he wasn't gonna be here next year." She wrapped her body around Ashton's ankles and tied his shoelaces together.

I could barely see Ashton under them. His feet kicked futilely. I let out a whoop and leapt on him too. The class cheered. Their bodies writhed all around me. We tore up Ashton's spreadsheets. I took his clip board and cracked it in half over his head. "Something is wrong here!" Ashton yelled. "Something is hideously wrong!" I told him if he kept starting sentences like that, his stipend would be withheld.

Alisha was the only one who received an "Adequate" on her assessment. I asked her to stay after class so I could give her a "Super Job!" sticker. She looked at it so intently I thought maybe she was praying. Then she said, "It's hard to be convinced of the necessity of verb tenses when our situation exhibits so little possibility for change."

I said, "Education is the number one predictor of economic mobility."

She picked at the sticker and whispered, "When I'm born, I am poor. Today, I am poor. When I die, I am poor."

"When I was little," I told her, "I thought that people who desired to do good things would accomplish good things. I thought that the best way to rectify evil was to notify the authorities. I thought there was nothing you couldn't understand if you were willing to ask questions."

"I thought if you had a brother in lockup with a hard rep, people would be too scared of him to rape you."

I gave her another sticker. "At this point," I said, "I don't scream, because I know if I started screaming I would never stop."

Devin's tooth was getting worse. When he spoke, gray foamy sludge spilled over his lips. I told him to open his mouth so I could look at it. His mouth had become a huge eroding cavern. His teeth were icebergs collapsing into a dark sea. As I watched, more fell away and the abyss enlarged.

I recoiled and went back to teaching poetry. Because I was on probation I had to read from the preapproved curriculum script to make sure that I didn't teach anything wrong. The Vice Principal checked on me every half hour.

"There are four types of poetry," I read. "Haiku, quatrain, acrostic, and limerick."

Thompson raised his hand and I called on him. He grinned. "I got a question, Ms. X. I'm sorry, but do you think Nacai smells like ass?"

The class howled.

"That's not following the Golden Rule, Thompson."

"My bad, my bad. But it's true, right?"

"Fuck off, Thompson," said Nacai. He was sitting in the back of the room and his voice was very small.

"Don't talk to me," said Thompson. "I don't want nobody talking to me who shit their pants."

"You are not showing respect to your peer," I told Thompson. "I'm going to write you up."

"Why don't you write up the person who shit their pants, is what I'm wondering?"

Nacai stood up and flipped his desk over. The Vice Principal walked in. The class screeched like an aroused monster with many heads.

"This is highly unorthodox!" shouted the Vice Principal.

I said, "Haiku is composed of three lines. The first line consists of five syllables. The second line consists of seven syllables. The third line consists of five syllables. Now let us look at this example poem about the snow goose."

I did not look at the Vice Principal. I only looked at the paper. If I looked up at the class they would become a sea and drown me.

The home test kit revealed two lines. I didn't believe it. I was sure there was a testing error. Maybe there had been some sort of irregularity in the test-taking environment. Maybe the proctor had been incompetent. I took another and another and another.

In the classroom I shattered my SUPER TEACHER! mug on the floor and said, "I'm pregnant."

"Oooh, bay-bee!" The class was thrilled.

"I call godmother!" yelled Lani.

Thompson yelled, "Don't worry, Ms. X, I'll teach your baby do the running man. S'gonna be tight."

"You don't understand, I can't bring a child into this world." They didn't understand. Every day children flooded into the world around them. They were foam on a rising tide. "I need to get rid of it."

That they understood.

"What my sister does is fall on her bicycle."

"You gotta drink bleach, Ms. X."

"You gotta shove some papaya up in your business."

Alisha dragged a chair to the front of the classroom. "Jump off your desk, Ms. X. Fall on this chair. It's the best way."

The class clustered around me. I stood on my desk. I jumped and crashed down onto the chair. A tree of pain unfurled in my stomach and I sobbed as the class applauded.

I climbed onto the desk again. Blood ran down my legs. My head was buzzing. It sounded like a million people were running toward me from very far away. I looked down at the children and saw their faces flecked with my blood.

"If the world were as I dreamt it," I told them, "I would be ten feet tall, waving a flaming sword." The million people were getting closer. "I would lead a horde of righteous warriors howling down a green hill." The world was growing translucent. "I would burn everything until you got what you deserved."

Suddenly we heard a thump on the window. The million people had arrived. It was everyone who had ever died for no reason. They were flinging themselves against the outside of the school. Their bodies were decaying and falling apart.

There was clamor in the hallway. The dead people had gotten inside. I could hear the Vice Principal yelling. "Do you have a hall pass? Do you have a hall pass?"

His voice made the pain bloom again in my stomach. I couldn't breathe. His shoes clicked closer to my door. I gasped, "There's no way out."

Alisha stepped forward. "You need to jump into Devin's mouth," she told me. Devin obligingly opened his mouth and I saw an endless black chasm.

Some of the class ran to the windows and flung them open. "Come in!" They beckoned to the dead people. "Hurry up!"

I looked from Alisha to them and back again. The Vice Principal was almost here.

Alisha said, "You need to jump like you would jump from a burning building into a fireman's net. You need to jump into Devin's mouth, otherwise this is the end and the stories will all be rewritten and there will be no sound left to speak our names."

The Vice Principal flung open the classroom door. "I spent six weeks at the National Summer Academy for Vice Leaders!" he shouted. "And before that I was a very successful hedge-fund manager! And let me tell you—*there does not appear to be a lot of learning occurring here!*"

His face shone with sweat. Dead people pressed close behind him. I jumped.

The gulf of Devin's mouth yawned around me. I didn't land. The class jumped behind me, one by one. Devin jumped last. "This way!" he called to the dead people. "Follow us!"

The light of the classroom shrank above us and vanished. The bottom was nowhere in sight. Black wind ribboned sweetly through our hair. The kids grabbed each other's hands the way they had been taught in kindergarten. We flew through the darkness toward a new world, and the dead poured down all around us.

Blood, Blood

I'm sixteen when George and I figure out the aliens will pay to watch us fight. We're leaning against milk crates in the alley behind the library and he's giving me shit about losing my waitressing job. To shut him up I bring my fist back in slow motion and plow my knuckles into the side of his mouth. He does an exaggerated, drawn-out reaction, flapping his lips out and staggering into the cinder block. Then at the last moment he spins, catches me around my waist, and pulls me in to him. My foot snags the milk crates and the stack comes clattering down.

A group of aliens are leaving the library—a family, maybe, if families are something they have. They catch sight of us—smell us, sense us, whatever—and drift over to the mouth of the alley. I feel George tense as the aliens say, What are you doing? What does this mean?

His face is drawing tight with irritation when I reach back and tickle him. My fingers dig into the softness between his ribs hard enough—maybe—to leave bruises. We topple to the pavement. He lands on top of me. His elbow jams my boob. Or, as my mom would say, the place where my boob ought to be.

"Shit, ow."

"So says the weaker sex."

"I hate you."

His whisper hums against my neck. "I know."

I flip out of his grasp and my knee drags along pavement, leaving a stain of capillary blood on the faded asphalt and the tufts of grass that break through.

How thrilling, the aliens murmur. How visceral.

A moment later George lies on his stomach. His feet kick feebly, like a turtle. "Mercy, fair lady!"

Sitting on his back, I inspect my nails. Each capped with a rind of black grime. Sweat, his and mine, soaks through my Stray Cat Diner polo.

"Mercy!"

When I let him up, he picks his messenger cap off the pavement. Dusts it off. Drops his card in and waves it toward the cluster of aliens. "Donations? Donations! Show your appreciation, whatever manner you feel is right."

Giggling, the aliens reach in and touch his card. Credit rushes into his account.

Even after they've paid him, they linger. They are fascinated by the way he grips the brim of his cap, the way I press my finger into the scrape on my knee and hiss as the sting flares and fades. George and I stand very still. Usually aliens don't leave unless you've really done nothing for a minute or two. They hate missing anything.

When they've gone, George flips them the bird. He checks the balance on his card and looks up at me, his mouth spreading into a grin. His eyes are hard and bright with opportunity. "We're rich."

I tell my parents that waitressing interfered with my schoolwork. The thought of this is so horrific that my mother drops the dust cloth and runs to smooth my hair. "Don't worry, honey, you do whatever you need to do. Eyes on that scholarship, right?"

"Sure, Mom. Whatever."

Really, Mr. Reade fired me for not being welcoming enough toward aliens. "I don't give a damn how you feel, Damia," he said. "We need them. They want to go behind the bar, you let them. They want to get right up next to people and watch them put fries in their mouths, you let them. Anything they want, you let them. Understand?"

I said I understood, but I couldn't help it. When one of them got near me, I froze up. I could hear my heart lurching, big as a cantaloupe, filling my whole torso. I was sure they could hear it too.

Sometime before the aliens found us, they discovered a way of divorcing their bodies from their minds. In cartoons and commercials here, the alien bodies are portrayed floating in pods of translucent goo, humanoid forms with wires running into them, rows of thousands upon thousands. The reality, I'm sure, is something totally different, something totally beyond any portrayal we might attempt.

Earth is visited, then, only by alien consciousnesses. They move through air, through concrete, through steel and polycarbonate with equal ease. They speak, or rather do not speak, in streams of thought directed toward our minds. Look at one straight, it's like the sunlight that plays on the hull of a boat in a lake. Only no boat, no lake, no sunlight.

Whatever splits them from themselves is not the only technology they have. They dole progress out to us in small doses. Cheap and infinite energy sources. Cures for genetic disorders. Earth governments turn into throngs of men clustered hungrily around the alien portals. Slowly now, the aliens say. You'll ruin yourselves.

Recently, reluctantly, they have agreed to take a small number of people each year back to their ship (or wherever they come from). The people will study alien technology so that it can be more unobtrusively incorporated on Earth. They will get to leave their bodies behind and move as pure consciousness. An alien came to our school to discuss the opportunity with us. If I hadn't been taking notes so frantically, I might have been unnerved at how silent the classroom was, the lecture delivered straight into our heads. But I was too busy panicking that I wouldn't get every thought down.

Halfway through the talk something hit my hand and made me start. George's copy of the brochure on alien exchange, folded into a paper football.

George doesn't mention his new source of income to his family. His mother and his sisters, they take what they can get, no questions. George's father split a long time ago, part of a NASA division to study alien tech. Or that's what he said. He also said he'd send them funds every month, enough alien credit to take a bath in. All they get is the government checks.

We've been friends since we were seven. At the beginning of third grade, this asshole Ross Tate followed us around for a week, singing "George and Damia, sitting in a tree—"

Punching Ross Tate was how I began my long and tumultuous relationship with in-school suspension.

Two days into my first suspension, I heard from another kid in the slammer that Ross Tate's desk had exploded. Firecrackers. He and three other kids ended up in the ER. The principal found a note in Ross's cubby, saying he had a plan to blow up my desk. He spelled my name wrong—D-a-m-Y-a. Tate spent a week in the hospital, and then two weeks in out-of-school suspension, crying about how he had no idea what happened. George's extralegal career was always more calculated than mine.

The aliens have no gender. When we asked them about it, they laughed and told us it was irrelevant. But it feels so strange to call a thinking being "it." "It" is more general than one being. We use the word all the time: It was irrelevant. It feels so strange.

Just in front of the Bean in Chicago, a patch of shimmering air hangs at eye level. If you walk straight at it, you can't miss the glint. If you come at it from the side it nearly disappears. Mostly people give it some space, though you could touch it, I guess. Every now and then, a bulge appears in the shimmer. It swells and grows and finally detaches, a scrap of light that floats away across Millennium Park. It's an alien, just arrived through the portal from shipside.

They could drift from shipside all the way to the surface of Earth, but it would take a long time. Or something. We're not totally clear where they come from, or how they perceive time. At some level, we assume, they value convenience.

They have no interest in the Grand Canyon or Everest or Victoria Falls. They put their portals in places where people gather. Parks, gas stations, fish markets. When we bump into each other or high-five or blow our noses, their delight is palpable. They've been here ten years and it's still unsettling. Sometimes when aliens follow George and me as we walk down the street, he will spin around. Flail his arms. Shout, "What! What are we doing?"

Those times, he might as well be talking to air.

When I was in elementary school a fun thing to do was play alien. Little mirrors or LED screens glued all over our clothes, reflecting back our surroundings and scenes from music videos. We stood stiffly in corners, flitted down the halls. Asked everyone, Did you see me? Was it like I wasn't there?

In high school it would be grotesque to be so overt. We still try to mimic them, though no one would admit it, and maybe no one could say exactly how it's done. Starving yourself is not the answer. The boniness of an emaciated kid is completely different from the gossamer presence of an alien. It's more a way of holding your body. A way of sliding your feet as you walk and knowing how the light falls on your face.

I wonder if the aliens can tell when we try to mimic them. If they coo over us in private. How flattering. How cute.

George sticks to coyer, anachronistic forms of rebellion. George grows his hair long. George wears all black. George pierces the protrusions of his flesh ("You have no idea how many aliens were in that tattoo shop") and fills the holes with metal studs. George stands in the middle of the football field and kisses boys.

One day we're sitting outside the library after a fight, holding matching ice packs to our faces. George leans back. "I don't get it. Why would anyone want to leave their body? It's part of you. It is you." He flexes his fingers as he says this, clenches his fist. As though whatever anchoredness he feels from these gestures will pass to the rest of the world. He cannot mentally separate himself from his body. I'm jealous.

"It's the stupid aliens making people think like this," he says. "They're making people go crazy."

"No." I press my lips together. "People thought this way before. We just never had an answer until the aliens came."

"It's a new thing to do. That doesn't mean it's an answer. That doesn't mean we've got the problem right."

A few days ago, George shaved himself a mohawk. He dyed it bright green and spiked it up with a glue stick. He has gold glitter on his face. His nails are painted bright red.

"How about this problem," I say. "I can't debate you when you look like a Christmas tree from Satan."

He pushes his ice pack into my face and I bite it and condensation trickles down my throat.

. . . .

My father is an insurance agent. At the same firm, his father before him. They sat behind the same cherrywood desk and took seriously the business of keeping people safe. On one side of his desk there's a framed picture of my mother and me at the beach. Also a drawing I made when I was four, of a horse with human hands.

But the aliens have made health care cheap and technology safe and hardly anyone gets sick anymore, anyway. My father was never laid off—the aliens grow stern at the idea of people losing their livelihoods. But there are mornings when I leave for school and he is frozen at the sink, bathrobed, staring out the window. There are afternoons when I come home and wonder if he's moved.

He buys cookbooks. He watches the Food Network. He says he will become a gourmet chef, which was always his dream. I come home from school and make us tomato and cheese sandwiches. I say, Daddy, how about we watch something different for a while? He nudges the remote over to my side of the couch.

My mother substitute-teaches and cleans. She pretends she cannot hear him when my father asks, could she turn off the vacuum for a while? She sets her body between him and the TV, vacuums around each of his feet in their slippers as though he were an ottoman she'd rather not touch.

At night I peel off my gym shorts and T-shirt and stand in front of the bathroom mirror. My lips, too big for my face. My breasts, too small. It puzzles my mother, who has said twice in the past year, I don't understand it, Damia, all the other women in our family have gorgeous bods. I think she's trying to comfort me. I guess it could be worse if she said, I do understand it, Damia. You got exactly what you deserve.

My hips are too wide compared to my waist. The pores on my nose are visible from several feet away. My hands are huge, like a man's, like a giant's. The curve of my shoulders—no, the hulk of my shoulders—is abhorrent. It's weirdly satisfying, this rephrasing of my body into something grotesque. So when I finally peel off the whole thing, it will be deserved.

I slap water onto my face and tell myself to quit wallowing. I'm lucky. Other girls born at other times didn't get my choice. Write three essays, get two teacher recommendations, take a test, drop into the goo (if we choose to believe the cartoons). You're wrong, George. We've all always wanted this. To have the doubts fall away. Everything and nothing. Reborn. Glory-blinding.

I tell George I have to make up a comp-sci quiz, and I linger after school. There's an alien in the guidance counselor's office. Is it the one who told us about the exchange program?

I am, it says. You are interested?

"Uh, yeah. Yeah, I am."

Please, sit down. Or, actually— In the fluorescent light of the office, the alien is almost invisible. A dime of dull air rather than a plate-sized shimmer. —would you like to go outside?

Under a tree in the school courtyard, the alien says, First, let me try to dissuade you.

"Dissuade me?"

Yes. This program—I'm not sure it's entirely a good thing. We don't fully know what the effects will be. And your way of life has been in balance for so long. It's a terrible thing to disrupt.

"You don't think you've already disrupted a lot?"

Its response is not quite words this time, only shades of discomfort, regret, defensiveness. I have to backtrack. "I'm sorry. I get it, definitely. But I've been thinking about this for a long time. I've made up my mind."

The alien's projection morphs into acceptance. Well. If you're sure. I've always said what independent minds you have. You'd be doing a great service for your planet, certainly. What's your address? I'll send you the application file.

George is smoking outside the old gas station and when I get there he says, "Jesus, that took a long time."

"Don't tell me. I'm shit at writing code." I focus on his shoes, the scar on his elbow, the cobwebby gas pumps. Not his eyes.

He knocks on my door when I'm working on my application, and I let my mother answer. I can't see her but I can picture her with her arms crossed, filling up the doorway, lips bunched in a disapproving rose. "You two seem to get hurt a lot, don't you?"

"The fuck, Damia?" George yells through her like she's a screen door.

His voice makes the bruise on my thigh, the scrape on my knee, the split on my cheek throb angrily. My fingers hang frozen over the keyboard until he's gone.

. . . .

It's the afternoon after I submitted the application, and the aliens are asking for another fight. George sits on the curb, scuffing gravel into a pile and not looking up.

"Oh, come on, guys. You're good for business. Wouldn't believe how good." Mr. Reade, my former employer. He likes us to beat each other up in the parking lot beside the Stray Cat. "They come from shipside talking about you," he tells us. "One of them called it—wait, wait, I got it—something like, 'an authentic celebration of human physicality.' That great or what?"

George snorts. "As long as they keep putting money in the hat."

"Hat? They're putting you in a guidebook."

There's a sucking shrinking feeling in my chest. I edge toward George to sit down beside him, but without warning he kicks one leg out and swipes my shins. My palms smash into the grainy asphalt. The shrinking feeling is knocked out of me, replaced by something clean and pissed off. I take a deep breath and sweep gravel at George.

"Bitch!" He clutches his eye. "Rocks? Seriously?" Then he stands, brings his hands up, bounces on the balls of his feet. "Okay, cheater. Let's do this."

"What I'm talking about," says Mr. Reade.

The alien running the exchange program tells me its name is Lute. Or at least, it puts something in my head, and out of the jumble I get that word. Pretty, melodious name. Genderless as always. Lute says it came here to get away from responsibilities at home. Sometimes, when they talk about back home, the idea that fills me is "another dimension." Other times I only get "shipside." I put the two ideas to Lute. Were they different places? No, no. I feel Lute's patient smile. They are two slightly different ways of referring to the same place. Epithets. The distinction grows wider in translation.

I wonder what it's really saying. I suppose there's no way to know. "Understanding" is predicated on having the same apparatus translate things in the same way. One mouth must translate thoughts to sounds in the same way that other ears translate sounds to thoughts.

But Lute! Lute is sunlight falling on dust. Our apparatuses might not even lie in the same dimension. I am so lucky that it can move through things as it does, bypass organs altogether. It lays down its intentions on my brain, and I give them meaning. The right meaning, I hope, though probably not. Inside the gnarled clod of my brain, something is always lost.

George shows up at my house one evening, looking like he's going to puke.

"My mother. Overdrew her card. Needed cash. Told the aliens they could come and watch her pay bills. Watch her boil pasta." Something jumps in the soft skin under his left eye. "Those morons would tip to watch me shit."

"Maybe she deserves a break." I put my hands around his forearm. Whatever anchoredness I feel, let it pass to you. "Really. How's it different from what we do?"

"That's a performance," he gasps out. "We can shuck that off. This is who she is."

"Right. She's a broke lady."

"She's a whore." He clutches my hand. Squeezes my knuckles white.

"And you're a terrible person." I go to flick him on the forehead, and somehow my hand doesn't fall away. Two of my fingers rest on the line of his jaw. His hands have moved up my arm now. His thumb brushes the inside of my elbow. He has been staring out at nothing but now his eyes move to me. And I fall in.

"You know, I don't think you're gay." I'm trying to make a joke. "At best you're an asshole." Then I kiss him.

His lips are dry and his hands move across my shoulders, down my back, over all the places where he has opened cuts on me and seen them heal and opened them again. All the places I wish different, that I do not like, gouged or no. His hands never break away.

Somehow my sports bra is over my head and his jeans are coming off. Oh, I think, it's so simple. Simple as throwing that first punch. These barriers between people, these gulfs, how easily everything collapses.

There's a moment, later, when I revise: Really, that was not like fighting at all.

A cross section of how we are, George and I. My blood, my skin, some air, his skin, his blood. Sometimes: blood, skin, air, wall, air, skin, blood. During sex: blood, skin, skin, blood. As close as we can get and seeking closer. But that final, perfect closeness?

Blood, blood? That's not a place we can get, no matter how deep we pull. We strain against the boundaries of skin.

Except sometimes, when we fight. My knuckle into his lip, just the right way. The gouge in his elbow knocking the scab off my ear. Blood, blood.

We get there.

There is the night we lie against each other, naked, when George freezes, breath trembling in his throat. "Do you think— this—would they pay to see—"

I kiss him hard, but the thought is already out. It hangs like a marble on a string between us and grows foggy with our breath. Yes.

Is the answer. We both know and the marble grows bigger and presses a red welt into my chest. Yes.

Not only would they, but they will and they have and they probably are. Just because this thing is newly discovered to us doesn't mean it isn't old and tarnished to plenty. And plenty who wanted to eat or wanted to please could so easily say: You want human bodies? You want flesh? Come this way.

Not prostitution, exactly. No give and take of pleasure. Just watching. They would take the same kind of joy in it that they take in watching cashiers scan groceries, girls play clapping games, men fix a roof. Could sex still have beauty if it took place under such bland, curious eyes? Could it still have cruelty if that horror was supplanted by the blunt horror of being observed? Meanings warp, meanings dissolve. But still we let them in. Into the most Eleusinian mysteries, even when it breaks our hearts. The marble, giant now, weighs on my lungs and makes it difficult to breathe. Why is it never us, I wonder. Why are we never the ones who get to smile, to say—No, this is not for you. It's complicated. In a million years, you could not hope to understand.

One night, my father asleep in front of the television, I hear the newscaster say, "With us tonight, Johanna DeWitt, first human to return from shipside. If you think the studio looks emptier than it should, don't worry! Johanna has undergone the splitting process. On the street you'd be hard-pressed to tell her from your average alien. Tell us, Johanna, how are you feeling?"

Johanna's responses scroll as text along the bottom of the screen. They angle the studio lights so that we can see her shimmering a foot above the couch. Another woman sits next to Johanna. The caption on the screen informs us that this is Helene, Johanna's wife. She is small, with a round face. Her eyes look straight ahead but down, maybe at the cameraman's shoes.

The Johanna scroll informs us that she and Helene met in graduate school, that they devoted their lives to alien tech, that they were both so overjoyed when Johanna was selected as an ambassador. My body is safe, Johanna assures us. And I feel so indescribably free.

Helene hunches her elbows in, as though trying not to occupy the space that Johanna's body would need, if Johanna were there. She twists her wedding ring.

George comes up to me after school, squinting, hands jammed in his pockets.

"So, do you . . . should we go on a date, or something?"

I burst out laughing almost too hard to gasp out, "No."

"Thank god." Tension relinquishes his shoulders.

"But—want to swing by the library?"

That means, want to punch me until my skull rattles, but we never say that. The fights exist in a new vicious language, modulated by the color and spread of our bruises. Since we both speak it there's no point in translating.

If you could lay your thoughts down on my brain, George. What would I understand?

When either of us lands a solid hit on the other there is a ripple of excitement among the aliens. My elbow goes into George's stomach and I can almost hear the chimes of their thoughts. Like starving men watching someone eat, I think. George hears it too. He clutches his stomach, his mouth frozen in the shape of pain. After a moment he catches my eye and grins, hard and grim.

I lean into his blows. Each punch he lands unmoors me a little more. If I can turn every inch of my body to bruise. Convert the entirety of my flesh to pain. Then by default the mysterious points of anchor will sever. I will rise into the air.

When I sit down to dinner with blood crusted around my nose, my eye puddled purple and yellow, my mother stares. My father saws at his chicken without putting any pressure on the knife. My mother swallows. "We could buy you some new foundation," she says.

Protestors grow more active in the wake of Johanna's appearance. Will we let them disembody a generation of our children?

No, we will not! Protect our human heritage! There are rallies around alien portals. A protestor grows wild, shoves his arm with his middle finger extended through the rippling air. His body convulses in a shudder—delight or anguish?—and he falls to the ground. They revive him with Gatorade and Cheetos.

I want to tell George how funny it is, the protestor slurping down Blue Ice, with dangerously cheesy dust around his mouth. Protect our human heritage! But George is not in school. He's not slouching behind the library or riding the kid swings at the park and drawing dark looks from the nannies. Four days go by.

I wake up feeling the imprint of his head against my chest. Every glimpse of dyed hair or glitter makes my heart lunge. I even try his mother's house and she says, "I'm sorry, who are you?"

The Chicago portal is destroyed. An organized act of terrorism, say the newscasters. No simple firecrackers either; they used alien technology. Set fire to the air inside a tightly controlled ring and devoured that unfathomable field. There's nothing there in the morning when the cameras arrive. A crowd gathers in the shadow of the Bean, unwilling or unable to believe that it is gone. For the first time in a long time they are actually staring at empty air.

The camera sweeps across the flock of faces and my heart flips so hard I can hear the deafening clap in my ears. There in the crowd, a green mohawk. His arms are crossed over his chest as he stares at the spot where the portal used to hang. His smile is hard and grim.

. . . .

I knew something would happen, says Lute. It and I are in the park. I sit with my back against a beech, a knot digging into my spine. We should not have given so much so quickly. You could not deal with it.

"No," I say. "It's not that. Not exactly."

Lute is puzzled but I keep silent. They get our actions. Our angers, even. But not our reasons. Not this time.

Finally Lute says, In any case we should hurry things along. I know officials shipside. They could bump you to the front of the list.

Its presence is pale, diffuse. In my mind I catch fragments of distaste, anger that softens to grief. The sun is a low yolk in the sky. There is an ant crawling up my calf. Across the park two kids are trying to ride their Big Wheel bikes down the grassy hill. At the bottom they catch, go flying off, and for a moment their long shadows leap away from their feet.

Lute says, Could I—do you think—can I touch you?

I know Lute doesn't truly mean "touch," but I know it does mean "front of the list." And the front of the list means escape. Certain definitions can be made hazy. Some lines can be blurred. The change in density that marks the boundary between my skin and the air can be bridged. Touched.

My heart races. I pick at the gummy lines of my cuticles. My wide hands with their bulging knuckles. The loaves of fat lying under the skin of my thighs. I could never have to look at this body again. I could never have to breathe.

So I say, "Yeah, sure." Lute is a patch of air in front of me, and then is not. Lute is now the length of my forearm. My flesh glows if I watch from the corner of my eye but fades if I look straight on. Lute moves up my arm and through my torso. Lute is a gentle orb of heat, or else a chill that ripples through me. Lute is saying, Wow, wow, wow.

Deep inside my head I picture my consciousness as a hot-air balloon, harlequin red and blue and gold. It strains against a hundred ropes. One by one they are struck through with an axe. The balloon trembles. Its basket tips back and forth.

Vessel. The word jumps into my mind, so derisive it scorches my hair. *Vessel.* Now I am open to the mockery of late-night talk-show hosts, politicians, mothers who gossip at luncheons. They don't know it, but when they say it, *vessel*, they are talking about me. Imagine it, being probed by the unknown. Being . . . occupied. Their disgust tinged with the heat of fear.

Vessels hand over not just actions but the medium of flesh. It's what the aliens most want. It gives them bragging rights shipside. They tell horror stories of their close encounters with bodies. Their friends listen raptly, the ones who would never be brave enough to come down here. They think, shuddering, of their own bodies, wherever they have left them. When they sleep (or whatever) they have dreams (or something different) of being trapped.

I tell myself that this new kind of revulsion is just a temporary burden. I tell myself guilt is just another trapping of flesh. My body senses that its time is almost up and so it casts out wild nets of feeling, trying to trap me and haul me back in. When I wake up retching at three a.m., sure that the gentle orb of heat has returned, that it has come through my neighborhood and my walls and my sheets to slide again up and down through my body, that's just muscle memory. Not a part of me.

And when I have no container? When I am no container? I will be nothing but myself.

I get out of bed and stand in front of the mirror. I cup a hand between my legs, cover everything up. I lay my other forearm over my breasts. More acts of self-censorship. Neuter. Neutral. It. *It* feels so strange. This is *it*.

George shows up at school the next Monday. He sits in the back of class with his head on the desk and the teachers don't bother calling on him. He ignores me at lunch. I stake out his locker after school but he doesn't pass by and by the time I've figured that out and sprinted from the building he's halfway down the street. He freezes when I shout his name.

I catch up to him and spin him around by the shoulders. It's disconcerting how much he looks the same. What did I expect, some disfiguring scar? A brand on his forehead? Whatever words I had desert me.

He speaks instead. "You applied for exchange." It's not a question. And now his face is falling apart. "All those times—you said you hated them. You said how stupid they were."

Oh, George. You are not the only betrayer here. How can I explain that yes, I said that. But more than those things, I want to fly and I want speak in the music they speak and I want to touch and be touched the way they are. He would say they had tricked me. He would look at me with pity, and when pity didn't change my mind it would change in him to disgust. But it's my right to want those things. It's a want that is in myself, not my flesh.

He's not done. His voice cracks. "How can you hate yourself that much? How—you would go somewhere you're not even sure exists. You would leave your own body. And me."

You've already left me, I want to say. Not in the same way that I would leave, but it's your way and it's as real to you as my way is to me. You know it is.

"Day. There are other ways to escape. We're fighting them. You should join us."

Join. The word could mean so much more. The meaning he intends for it is sad, inadequate.

But the impossibility of that word brings me up short and grief bells inside me. I want to stave off that truth as long as possible. I lean forward and kiss him, clutch him to me. Suddenly it doesn't matter whether the desire is in my flesh or in my mind, whether our words are adequate or not, whether everyone on the street is staring at us. Stay with me.

He pushes me off. "Fuck's sake. Sell yourself to the devil, sure. At least stand by your own position. This is pathetic."

Words calculated to smart. Words to reach where blows cannot. Where bodies refuse to go. They dig a honed edge into my chest and all the reasons why I can't lose him spill out like organs. I clutch my stomach—the points of anchor will be severed—and turn, and flee.

. . . .

I plow through my house, upstairs into my room, punch the wall. Hot tears bully their way out from under my eyelids. Stupid girl. Typical girl. Crying because I would lose a boy I loved. Because my body was something people looked at as an artifact, and I was trapped inside it.

My mother comes into my room holding the computer. She sees me slumped on the rug and kneels down next to me. "So you've heard."

I have no idea what she's talking about.

"You got a letter. From the regional exchange office." She hands me the screen.

In light of recent terrorist attacks, the alien bureau regrets to announce that all scholarship exchange programs will be put indefinitely on hold. We regret the inconvenience and hope that amicable relations can be restored with all possible speed.

Postscript—Damia, I'm really very sorry about this. —Lute

Behind their words I can feel it, really feel it, for the first time. The bafflement. The seeds that will blossom into disgust. The aliens rustle and murmur, After all we gave you. After all we sang your praises. How did we deserve that? How could you?

"Honey, I'm so sorry." Mom pats my hand. "I know how hard it is to feel you have nowhere to go."

But I drop the computer and ease out from under her palm. My eyes are dry. My nose isn't running anymore. I stand up and step into the doorway.

"Actually, I think I'm going outside."

I jog into the center of town and stand outside the Stray Cat. Aliens spill out of it, following the end of the lunch rush. Aliens everywhere, following shoppers, watching toddlers drop ice cream.

"You want to fucking understand?" I scream at them. "Come here." The humans who are around look up too and cover their babies' ears. Fuck that. "Put this in your fucking guidebook."

The aliens follow me. They call to each other in their incomprehensible music and more come pouring out of shops and houses and Starbucks. They flock behind me until I'm wearing a shimmering cloak of air that billows across the whole street.

I don't need to look more than one place. George. I know where you are.

I hope he gets my message, through my eyes and my set chin and my clenched fists. There are no more words between us. I will lay my thoughts down on his body, and he will give them meaning.

I round the corner of the library just as he's stubbing out his cigarette. He sees the aliens behind me, the flock, the exaltation, the avalanche. His eyes grow huge. I don't pause, just bring my fists up and heave myself into his chest. He catches me around the waist, eyes still wide. Yeah, this dance. Remember, George?

But he just pushes me back, barely any force, his lips parted in a silent question.

I slam my fist into the side of his face.

He staggers sideways, recovers. Bounces once on the balls of his feet and then lunges. Some restraint has been severed. Blows rain down on both sides of my head. He's stronger, he's always been stronger. He's a he, not an it. My head rings like a hundred aliens are screaming. A hundred aliens are screaming. There's something warm running through my hair. Lights in my skull explode. Light reflects off the sweat on his nose. I drop down, jut my shoulder into his stomach and feel his guts rearrange. He flips over my back, legs flailing, hits the asphalt with a noise of meat and wetness. I've always been faster. I'm a she, not an it.

The bar of his shin knocks my ankles out from under me and I drop. My head bounces on—softness. George's outstretched arm. My whole body peals with pain. Heartbeats flood my brain, drowning out the bray of alien projections. I can feel George's pulse through my scalp. His forearm is slickening with my blood. My body fills with the crashing of my breath, in and out and in. Dark arterial colors are leaching into my vision. I fight the encroaching haze, wrench my eyes into focus. Above us the sky is dazzling blue, and empty.

Sex Dungeons for Sad People

It's not that much of a mystery. It's a translucent, human-size latex bag. I take off my clothes and climb inside. They seal up the top. There's a rubber gasket that fits over my mouth so I can breathe. My lips are the only part of me that are exposed, which is why I have to wear lipstick but eye shadow is optional. Then they fit a hose onto a valve at the bottom and vacuum the air out of the bag. My arms get clamped to my sides. My legs get clamped together. They fasten the reinforced straps at the top of the bag to a hook in the ceiling and haul me up two feet, three feet above the floor. It's like I'm being hung from my skin but there's no pain. It's like my brain is sinking in a pool of cream.

I'm in the most exclusive room of Skin Tight; only Triple Deluxe Golden Venus members get this far. Sometimes it's executives on a spree but tonight it's a politician and some of his college brothers. That's all I know. On a table covered by a white cloth are laid out all the tools they can choose from, the vibrators and safety blades, the spark wands and the ice and the clamps. The rules are: no damage to the bag, no damage to the performer. There's always a watcher, somewhere, a window up high.

The latex quadruples every sensation. A tap on my shoulder blade radiates out through my whole back. Clients love it when I moan. They reach up to brush my lips. Sometimes they swing me back and forth like the meekest game of tether ball. Sometimes they rub their bodies against me. This politician loves the colored ice. He holds the cubes with silver tongs and slides them down my thighs. The cubes are made of something thicker and darker than water, and as they melt they leave trails of red and purple and green. The brothers paint me like a canvas and I cry out at the cold.

You would think I'd panic occasionally and writhe and claw at the bag. You'd think that but I don't. Even the first time I didn't. I'm good at not acting on every thought that goes through my brain. When the clients leave and they lower the bag and unseal it, I climb out with nothing to show but a thin film of sweat on my back. They dust the bag with baby powder to make sure I don't stick. It makes me smell dry and floral. When I get home Kevin cuddles me on the couch and strokes the insides of my arms. "This job, babe." He shakes his head like it's the darndest thing. "It makes your skin so soft. You're even softer than Flower."

On the floor Flower is busy with a pig ear but she thumps her tail when she hears her name.

. . . .

I met Kevin because he was an aide on Mom's ward in the assisted-living home. He was always the best at explaining things, what the new machine was for or why they had changed her dosages. He would text me at the end of his shift to let me know she was sleeping alright. I told myself it was kindness; he was a kind person, which was fine. But at some point I started to hear from him when he wasn't even at work, and eventually I was sending him the tiniest details of my life. *I got a paper cut under my thumbnail and it hurts.* Or, *I thought there was a bug in my hair but there's not.* Things I hadn't known I needed to tell someone. You go around for a long time carrying the minutiae of yourself in your own two hands, and it's not so bad, not even that heavy. It's just a thing you have to do. And then every so often a person shows up and opens their arms like the clean empty surface of a table, and suddenly your hands feel unbearably full, and you know that what was true isn't true anymore, you couldn't for another instant continue bearing so many small stories on your own.

One weekend night at Skin Tight gets me six hundred on an average evening, but that's not going to cover us plus Mom plus Kevin wants to do nursing school at night, so during the week I work in the seventh grade Alternative Learning Styles class of Stars & Stripes Collegiate Liberty Prep Academy. The school is an old strip mall in what I think used to be a bank building. Sometimes the kids have bake sales out of the drive-through teller window. Stars & Stripes hired me without explaining exactly what an Alternative Learning Style was, and I'm still trying to figure it out. For example, as far as

I can tell, Champagne's learning style is mimicking the sounds of technology at earsplitting volume. Or Brooklyn's learning style is furtive, relentless masturbation. Or Jolie's learning style is whales.

Today in the classroom they're supposed to be reviewing the origins of supply-side economics, but Champagne keeps twisting around so her head is under her seat and her butt sticks up in the air. "It *hurts,*" she says. Mr. K tells her to sit up and she does but then she puts her hands in the air, signing *bathroom* and clicking the phlegm around in her throat so it sounds like typing keys.

Eventually Mr. K lets her go, and she does a funny twitching hop across the room and into the bathroom. The class is focused again and Mr. K tries to get them to identify a man's picture on the Smartboard. They're guessing Hawkeye or John Cena or maybe Rainbow Dash so Mr. K has to do three claps for silence before he says, "Actually, this is John Maynard Keynes!"

There's a crash from the bathroom. The kids jump and Prius says "Cleanup in aisle five!" in a perfect loudspeaker imitation. When I get into the bathroom I find Champagne on the floor with her uniform pants around her ankles, flailing like a beached mermaid. She makes a high insistent noise like a carbon monoxide alarm and claws at her hips. Her Minnie Mouse underpants are probably four sizes too small. The elastic is stretched as tight as wire. It digs so deeply into the flesh of her legs there are bright raw welts in her skin, and her thighs are blotching purple. She stops the alarm noise long enough to look at me with deep-welling eyes. "It *hurts.*"

I go back into the classroom. "She's stuck in her underpants," I tell Mr. K.

He trails off from an explanation of the Laffer curve. "What?"

"Someone made her put on underpants that are too small. She's stuck."

He glances back and forth from me to the Smartboard diagram. "Jesus."

"They're hurting her. We have to cut them off."

"Oh no." He puts both hands on his jaw like something suddenly throbs. "No. We can't cut off a student's underpants."

"Well. She's not going to be able to pay attention."

Brooklyn raises his hand: "I have underpants."

Mr. K waves weakly at the Smartboard. He massages his eyelids. "Jesus." He looks up at me. "You have to do it. I can't go in there with her. They do not pay me enough for this."

Prius says, "Now available for three easy payments of nineteen ninety-five!"

Champagne is still trembling on the floor when I go back in. I lay her head in my lap. She makes a soft computer trill. I slide the blade of the scissors along her hip, between her skin and the underpants. Her trill grows a degree more urgent. I try not to prick her but just touching the welts makes her flinch. Champagne is big for twelve. Her flesh as it is freed from the taut elastic exhales with relief, rises into smoothness. I slice through the cotton on each of her hips and for a moment let her lie naked in my lap, trilling, her face buried in my skirt. I wash the welts with only water because she gets frantic at the sight of soap. I bandage them with gauze and tape because we have no Band-Aids big enough. I button her uniform pants. I buckle her belt. I pull her up off the bathroom floor and make her look at me. "Commando today, Cha-cha. It's no big deal."

She gives one forlorn beep but when I open the bathroom door she walks out first.

Marcus has booked my whole Friday evening at Skin Tight. Marcus comes in about once a month. He has one of those jobs that seems important if you don't really think about it. He wears rings but he never hurts me with them. Tonight he sits for a long time, cross-legged on the bamboo floor in his cashmere socks with his cheek against my calf. He clutches my toes as though I am some helium-filled woman who might at any moment fly away.

He tells me about his children, how his daughter cries and won't go to school. His wife wants to talk to specialists. He is afraid. I don't want her to feel like a failure, he says of his daughter. I don't want her to think that the way she is isn't okay. Does it mean I am a failure? Does it mean I am not okay? He and his wife have fought every night this week. He told her she was too ready to admit defeat. She told him he was willfully blind, too weak to ask for help, pathetic in his brute insistence of fine-ness.

I breathe loudly so he knows I'm listening. I don't speak for Marcus. Eventually he goes to the table and picks up the spark wand. He carries it to me, hovers its slender tip—like a candle flame shaped out of glass—a millimeter away from my stomach. I'm still, not like a dead thing: but like a thing absolutely in control. The spark wand whirs. For a moment we stay poised together on this pinnacle of need. Nothing so mysterious here, just a person who wants to not hurt anybody for a little while. He presses a button on the wand. A single thread of pink light leaps from it to me and I buckle like a fish on a line. There is nothing left in my head, not the sound of electricity popping across my stomach, down my thighs, only the pain like metal screws into the soft mesh of my nerves.

I wail and he jerks the wand away. Drops it on the table and presses to my body. His head between my breasts, his lips pressing through the latex against my sternum. "I'm not a failure."

It takes a moment for my nerves to unscrew. My tongue unlocks. I move it around inside my mouth and push saliva out to the tissue-papered skin of my lips. "No," I say to him. "No, you're not."

He nuzzles his nose against my chest. This is how I speak to Marcus. "No, you're not a failure. You work so hard. You're so smart. So smart. Such a smart boy. What a good, smart boy." With each sentence he mews and rolls his face across my torso. Presses his eye socket against the cushion of my upper arm. Presses his mouth against my ribs. "My good boy. I'm so proud of you. So proud of you."

He touches his temple to my clavicle but doesn't try to work his way any higher. Skin Tight has very carefully measured the height at which I hang. I am just high enough that even a taller-than-average man cannot reach my lips with his. So Marcus just stands with his head nestled into me, his arms wrapped around my body as though otherwise he might collapse. The latex by now has warmed, stretched between us like a second skin, though whether it is his or mine is no longer clear.

. . . .

You'd think my body would be crowded with memories of pain. You'd think that but it's not. At night I lie in bed with Kevin and feel only the cool of the sheet and the warmth of his skin. When we were first together we slept clutching each other like two lovers in a barrel going over Niagara, but in order for things to last they have to loosen. Now I sleep on my back with one arm stretched toward him, and Kevin sleeps on his stomach with his arm reaching over my chest. His fingertips just brush my breast.

The first thing I ever saw him do was count out pills for Mom. I couldn't take my eyes off the gentleness in his hands. Now there are times when I hate him so much that pale spots crowd my vision. I think of all the tiny things I know about him that no one else knows. I think of how benevolent I am, not to speak them out loud. Petty things, unfairnesses, low and spiteful snares. I want him to be grateful to me for not saying what I could say. I want him to walk to me on his knees and clutch my legs and lick the honey that leaches through my skin.

For example I could tell him that sometimes I let him help me with things and then I go back and fix them later. Or I could say, you are not as good at public speaking as you think you are. And also, I know your new haircut is supposed to be professional, but really you look a little like a Nazi.

I'm sure there are things he could say to me also, things I would not expect but that would wreck me. Open his mouth and there they are, my smallest fears laid naked on the table. All the things I imagine he doesn't even notice but of course he knows, of course nothing is hidden between us, we two goose-bumped patches of shadow with the dog sprawled vigorously over our feet. My heart swells inside me. There is only myself, protecting him from those hideous wounds. Only my frail and treacherous mouth. There should be a password, there should be a safety lock. Who would trust me with a job like that?

I assume that's what love is. To be bursting full of the most hurtful things you could say to a person, and not say them. And they lie inches away from you, not saying the things that could hurt you most. You hold that unbearable knowledge and you feel the heat radiating from each other's skin. Hello, hello, let me buy you breakfast. Let me rest my lips against your neck as though I were placing my head inside the mouth of a bear. You are the only missile, you are the only shield.

It's morning math in Mr. K's class and we're learning about compound interest. We make a big graph on the wall and use different colored markers to draw the difference between compounding continuously and compounding yearly. "Remember," says Mr. K. "When you're calculating payments, you need to specify both the frequency of compounding *and* the interest rate!"

Champagne today sits upright in her desk. She keeps sneaking looks at me, wiggling her eyebrows and mouthing the word *Commando.* I gesture at her to turn back toward her graph. Next to me Brooklyn tears up his worksheet and folds it into hard little needles and pokes them at my arm. He tells me about how Needle Man could kill me by throwing one of these into my neck at the speed of sound. Seychelles has just remembered a time two years ago when a fire engine drove by and scared her, so now she's started to cry. The assistant principal pokes his head in and tells Mr. K that during the night Jolie choked on her own mucus and died.

I'm across the room learning about Needle Man but I see Mr. K cross his arms very high on his chest. The assistant principal sees Seychelles crying and nods. "Oh, you've heard already."

I'm still not sure what they're talking about but I know it's something from how tightly Mr. K shakes his head. Brooklyn spears me again with his paper. "Invisible to the naked eye, but a single touch will *DESTROY YOU.*"

Champagne leans out of her chair to drum on the empty desk next to hers. "Mr. K, look, Mr. K? Jolie is *absent* today." Absent is a word they learned last Friday when we went over the school's new zero-tolerance attendance policy.

Finally Mr. K comes over and explains it to me and then we explain it to the kids. We let them leave their seats and wander around the room. They make doorbell noises and tap dance and eat their hair. They roll their faces against my body and mew. None of them ask me why. I'm glad because I don't know, but in the same way I don't know why Brooklyn's dad is in New Mexico, or why all the other students get fifteen minutes in the parking lot after lunch and they do not. When you get down to it really I think no one mystery is bigger than any other.

The funeral is at the big square church under the light-rail line. It didn't start out under a light-rail line but the church is old and the train is new. There are only enough pews to fill the front half of the church; the back half is filled with of folding chairs with metal seats sculpted in the imprint of a butt. The inside of the church is painted a peeling salmon pink that has faded to orange in the places where the window light hits it. I go to the bathroom and the toilets are low to the ground like they were meant for a kindergarten classroom. You don't have to say anything, believe me, I know there are places in the world that put beauty into their buildings and this isn't one of them.

Kevin is studying for an anatomy exam this week so I'm here alone. I go all the way to the back with Ms. Madison from Counseling and Ms. Astrid from the Creative Entrepreneurship Center. We sit on folding chairs, our knees in our polyester church pants lined up in a row. Up in the front the family files in, quiet people, their mourning clothes still creased from sitting so long in the back of the closet. This isn't a place of beauty, I know, but even in this church the salmon walls stretch up two or three stories high. You walk into even this church and you can feel the space between you and the roof opening and opening. You can sit with the great expanse of the air.

The minister up on stage looks like Kevin's baby cousin. He keeps his hands in the air most of the time like he hopes it will make him seem bigger. He has a lot to say about the things Jolie was spared from. She was spared from crack, she was spared from crank, she was spared from liquor, she was spared from ice. With each affliction spit out, his arms rise higher, his hands shake like he's trying to fling thick liquid off his fingers. She was spared from the clap, spared from the other clap, spared from the unspeakable scourge.

He tells us it isn't God's job to wake us up every morning. His eyes dart around above our heads like maybe he's looking into the spirit world, but I know what men's eyes look like when they rest on a miracle and that's not it. He's trying to tell us about how Jolie was spared the sins of teenagerhood, except he keeps calling her Julie and finally one of her uncles in the front yells out, "Jo-*lee.* Come on, man."

My eyes find Jolie's mother. From where I sit I can see only the perfectly arranged back of her head and a bare sliver of her cheek. When she came in for parent-teacher conferences last year she wasn't nearly so still. Going all over the room, picking up toys and putting them down. Had we *seen* her baby lately? Had we even *seen* the kind of *progress* she was making?

You'd think she'd be the kind of woman to howl and tear her hair, but she doesn't. The minister is spouting praise for being spared the foul lust of men, and Jolie's mother doesn't weep or shake or even look away. She only sits with her head tilted a little, like she's working to make sense of what she sees. The room is full of heavy salmon-colored air and I can't take my eyes off her. I realize hers is the truest sadness I have ever seen, and all the rest of us have only been pretending. My mouth wells with saliva. She is a state of matter different from everything else here, a vapor, a jet of steam. How can no one else be shaking in her presence? I want to crawl to her feet. I want to climb inside the cloud of her—withdraw all of my limbs into her concealing fog. I can't hear the minister's voice anymore. Every fluid in me is on the move. Come on, mama, I would say to her, get your harpoon gun, we can go hunting for God by ourselves, out on the wide open blue, we won't miss a thing.

I know, I know it's not any of my business. I'm good at not acting on every thought I have. I don't have reflexes; I have choices. They teach us that at Skin Tight.

So I choose to climb onto Astrid and Melanie's shoulders. They don't feel me; I am so light. I glide forward over the pews, stepping from one person's head to another like they're lily pads in still water. No one looks up, no one notices, all the way to the front of the church. I find Jolie's mama and lift her fingers with my fingers, both of us touching the other so lightly, just like we weren't even two bodies. She raises her eyes to me and then she dips her head.

I lead her out of the church and no one says a word. I lead her all the way to Skin Tight, through the dark doors, to the very back room. I face her, I touch her face, I so gently lift the blouse off her shoulders. We undress each other without ever brushing the other's skin. Together we step into the latex bag, and she wraps her arms around me as they pull it over our heads. I can feel her breathing; our lungs expanding and contracting in turn.

They seal the bag around us and remove all the extra air. From the outside the latex clouds our shapes so you can't tell where I end and she begins. My arms blur into her waist. Her nose merges with my neck. Inside the bag is sweet and warm, the fog of her breath on my skin, our breasts crowded between us. They raise us into the air so that we hang with only each other to hold. Two organs inside one skin.

Then the men come in. All the most valued clients of Skin Tight. Clean-shaven men with slicked-back hair. Men rolling up their shirt sleeves, loosening their collars. Men gently rubbing the tight muscles of their jaws. The men come in and as they enter they pass the table covered with a crisp white cloth. On the cloth there are crystal bowls, bowls filled with hundreds of cubes of red-dyed ice.

The men come in and they take up the red ice cubes and they walk toward us, me and mama, they walk toward us as though they are coming into church. More and more men crowd into the room, all with red ice melting on their fingers. They stretch their arms to our hanging bodies. They touch us with their ice. They slide the cubes along our backs, thighs, calves. They stripe us crimson. There are too many men to all reach us at once and so they have to take turns. Like boys turning their crayons to the walls they scribble on us, they draw graceful loops, they scrawl their initials and blot them out. They stroke us until every inch of our translucent skin drips red.

I don't twitch anymore at this kind of thing, but mama wails when the first touch of cold sears her through the bag. She wails purely, with an open mouth. I feel her hot gasps against my shoulder, her muscles spasming against mine. Even though outside they are so careful. These men who only want to not hurt anything for a little while. It's okay, I whisper. This is it. It doesn't really touch you. It feels like it does, but it doesn't. Even when the pain is so great you think it must leave you marked, or maybe you'll never emerge. Don't worry. You are whole. You keep on living. You arch your neck like this.

Her head collapses back.

You dig your nails in like this.

Her fingers gouge into my sides.

You breathe—like this—

You breathe, and you breathe.

Not an Alien Story

Creigh is sort of a moron and Marko doesn't give a shit so usually I'm the one in charge around here. We bunk in the same room of a temp house. Used to be a big box store, like a Kmart or something, but when those got shut down someone with entrepreneurial verve decided to rearrange the shelves like room partitions and charge a hundred bucks a month.

They make plenty of money off coastal people who get flooded out. The sea rise keeps on coming. Slides its big troll hands under town after town and squeezes.

After it squeezed Norfolk I left my dad and my little sister in Blacksburg where we had some relatives. The sister still had two years of high school left. I hadn't graduated but I turned eighteen so they wouldn't let me back in. I told everyone I wanted to look for a job because it sounded better than saying I wanted to get the fuck away.

I ended up in Akron, sitting in the cavernous dark of a warehouse, pretending I like these people.

Marko's cooking tonight. Pasta boiled on a Bunsen burner with American cheese melted in. Creigh sucks half-brewed beer straight out of the carboy. Creigh. You couldn't wait?

He burps. "Shit, man. What's the point of waiting?"

"We've got nothing to do but wait."

"Well I got nothing to do but drink wort."

Talking to Creigh makes you think he stole something from you. His head droops like one of those souvenir turtles with its neck hung from a string inside its shell. He's got bony arms and watery eyes and three older brothers, all of them dead.

Afterwards we sit around picking dinner out of our teeth. There's only windows in the front of the warehouse so stuff gets dark pretty fast. The ceiling is so distant you can hear wind blowing.

The evening sticks its nose under its tail. In a far corner of the store people are chanting. Someone shoots up a little bouquet of fireworks, *popopop*. Applause scatters through the warehouse like the wind rattling seed pods. I used to think you could get evicted for things like fireworks but now I can't imagine who would do the evicting. This whole place is going to burn down any day.

"Hey, Marko," I say, "why don't you tell us some stories?"

He turns his big boulder head toward me real slowly. I think his eyebrows would be knitting together but the unibrow's already got that covered. "Now why would you be asking me that, precisely, huh?"

Marko's from some island that got drowned under the sea rise. He moves like it's a waste of time. We're the same height but I always feel smaller, like my bones are bone and his are rock. I don't want him pissed at me but I really want to hear a story so I stay quiet.

Marko goes, "Is it because, maybe, I grew up on an island? And I sat around in my loincloth listening to the wise aunties tell fables about the seagull that shat out the world, is that it?"

Creigh drops his pointy body down between us and unfolds a secretary. Its light spills onto our faces. I don't know where Creigh got a secretary. He tries to jump on network and it murmurs, no signal, no signal.

Marko snorts. "Yeah right, man. They don't want driftwood jumping on."

Instead Creigh uses the secretary like a flashlight, spotlights my taped-up hand.

"Dammit, man. *Brutal.*" He glances at my face to check if I appreciate the sympathy.

I pick the bandage and try to look indifferent. "Yeah."

"Teach people to talk to Cheyenne, huh?"

Cheyenne is my ex-girlfriend. She lives in the front of the store. Creigh wants me to say *Damn straight* and high-five him, which irritates me.

"No. Look. The guy just looked like he was bugging her. So I steeled him. No story."

Creigh crumples a corner of the secretary screen between his fingers like a dog-eared book page. "It is a story."

"It's not."

Marko makes a *like hell* sound in his throat.

"That was really good macaroni you made tonight," I tell him.

"Fuck you, Asa."

. . . .

The next morning I go outside. The sky is a milky gray and the parking lot spreads out in front of the warehouse like a lake. Some kids have tied a bucket to one of the light posts and now they're playing a dumb version of basketball. Two girls and a boy. They leap and shoot and crash into each other with silent intensity. They play like people who put all their energy into their bodies because it's got nowhere else to go.

Some days something happens and it means the same thing your whole life is going to mean. It's weird how all the shit of a lifetime can get narrowed into a slice of hours. It's weird how the earth your home was built on can turn to silt, and one day you step on your carpet and it squishes.

Creigh stands in the service alley around the side of the warehouse. At first I think he's pissing but then I realize he's just staring at something, hands clasped in front of him.

"Whoa, man," he says. His Adam's apple bobs. "Whoa."

I look. It's a thing. It's about the size of a big watermelon, smooth and glistening. Fat at one end and then tapering down to a stubby flag that's maybe a tail. The body pulses gently. It's light pink, or else translucent, or else, I don't know, the color of clouds at dawn. Looking at it makes me confused.

"Creigh," I say, "are you afraid?"

"What?" he says.

"Are you hungover?"

"Oh." He flickers his mouth into a smile shape. "Ohmyfuggengod, yeah."

I bend down. On its fat end, the thing has a human face. Or at least a kid's drawing of a human face. Bulbous drooping nose and a grimacing mouth and flat gray dots that look like eyes but stare at nothing. I wave a hand at it. Hello? The face doesn't twitch.

It lies over a drainage grate in the service alley. Its sides flutter. I want to say it's breathing but it could easily be masturbating or dying or preparing to attack.

Marko walks up to us, thumbing the bristles on the back of his neck. "Jesus, Creigh. What did you hork up."

"No." Creigh shakes his head. He stares at the thing and bites his lip so hard his skin goes white. "It looks like a deep-sea creature."

"Deep-sea creature?" Marko steps back. "If it's a deep-sea creature we oughta pour gasoline on it and set it on fire. We oughta stake it down and pull its guts out and slice them into ribbons and fill its cavities with acid."

Creigh shifts his stare to Marko. "What do you have against deep sea creatures?"

"What do I have against deep-sea creatures?" Marko thumbs Creigh and turns to me. "What do I—Jesus. Can you believe this guy?"

"What would a deep-sea creature be doing in Akron?" I ask Creigh.

"What are we doing in Akron?"

I can't decide if this is idiotic or brilliant so I don't respond.

"What do we know?" Marko scuffs the gravel. "Maybe it's part of the native Ohioan fauna."

A fine net of red lines overlays the thing's pale body. Dancing red, brighter than blood. Around its bulging face they fade to a haze of rose, blackberry.

"Marko." I look at him. "That is. The stupidest thing. I've ever heard."

"Oh right, I forgot you're such an expert on Midwestern animals. I forgot about those nature walks you go on. Harry fucking Thoreau."

"It's Henry, and go suck a dick."

Creigh punches my arm. "Asa. I think it's hurt."

Now that he says it, there's definitely an urgency to the way the thing trembles. It makes me feel a pull like I'm horny or I've just been betrayed. Creigh squats down next to me. His knees stick out like a frog. He puts his face two inches from the thing. "I think we should take it inside." He doesn't touch it. He waits for me to move. There's a vapor of concern in his voice, the same pull, and it makes my caution fall away.

I scoop the thing into my arms. It's heavy but not dense, like holding an armful of cloud. A cloud made of pudding. Something beats inside it. Clear mucus soaks through my shirt. Its face remains immobile, glum. I kind of think it's not a face at all. Why does a face have to be a face? Could be its side, or its ass, or a mask.

We find a blue wading pool leaned up against the back wall of the warehouse. There's a lot of stock that got left here when the store shut down. Creigh dumps in three buckets of water.

"What? We didn't find it in water."

He shrugs.

I add a plastic pillow from a lawn chair and cover it with a towel. Like a dog bed.

Creigh sets in two cans of Natty Ice.

Marko stands back and watches us, his eyes and mouth small like lines scratched in a mountain. Then he jumps forward and drops in a Trudy Keane thriller.

"What're you on?" Creigh does his huh-huh caveman laugh, the one that makes me not want to be seen with him. "Thing can't read."

Marko stares at him. "You just gave it *beer*."

I say, "Even if it could read, Caliban, why would it know English? And why would it pick some splatterpunk pulp like Trudy Keane?"

Marko jabs a finger at the paperback. "Those books, they put me to sleep at night. Nothing else does."

I ease the thing into the wading pool. It lies in the shallow water, still trembling. Its expression hasn't changed. It looks nauseated. Creigh knocks the pool with his foot and the water sloshes and the thing's blubber sloshes with it.

We sit around the pool. Our eyes are stuck on the thing, its iridescent scum, the boundaries where its cloudlike body fades into the water.

"Maybe it's the mutant baby of a mad scientist."

"Maybe it's an alien from a planet where everything is made out of snot."

"Maybe it's a person who went through a time vortex and got turned inside out."

"Maybe it's Jesus Christ come back through a time vortex as a mutant alien baby made out of snot."

"Maybe it's someone's tumor."

Time swims through the emptiness of the warehouse. Maybe I should make us get up, but I don't. I wonder if something amazing is going to happen.

Eventually Creigh and Marko drift away. Creigh's got some girl. Marko I think is buying drugs.

People here don't really hang out with each other. There are the ones passing through, whom don't want to get to know you. There are the ones who have been here way too long, who you don't want to get to know. Then there are all the ones who don't know when they're leaving or where they're going. But none of us wants to admit that. We all smell like low tide.

We spend our days filling out job applications for the night shift in biofuel stations and demo crews. No one's hiring. We sit under overpasses and wait for religion to find us, but the roads are empty.

There's a metal staircase bolted to the side of the store so you can get up on the roof. One time I dragged a mat up and tried sleeping there, but I got all this black moss and roof tar on my blankets. I worry I'll have dreams about mildew, or about the people I love getting crushed in a whirlpool. You'd think these things would consume me. But I hardly ever dream.

You'd think more people would jump off the roof. Mostly they just stand and stare out. The view isn't great. Wheat fields, gray trees. Convenience stores and laundromats and self-storage parks with most of the units holding families. One day I can imagine standing up there, squinting at the seam of Earth and sky, watching the sea rise come over the horizon like cavalry.

Sea rise. What an idiot word for something so huge. But you can't call it a hurricane, or a tsunami. You can't even call it unexpected, since it just creeps up year by year. Sea rise. Like someone snuck in your house and cut your balls off, and then said, also, I'm sorry, but you can't live here anymore.

I think I'm going out but I end up kneeling by the wading pool again. The thing hasn't even rolled over. I plant my hands in the water. Cold laps at my wrists. I make fists and watch my knuckles rise out of the water like two archipelagos. Flatten my hands and they sink back down.

I lean in so close to the thing that my nose almost touches it. It smells like cold sweat. It shines like it's been cut out of some larger animal. I think about the shamans who licked toads and understood the future. I imagine my limbs flooded with visions of warmth and glory.

I press my tongue against its flesh.

Creigh says, "Asa?" and I leap up and splash water on both our shirts. He looks at me, then at the thing. He wants something so badly that I can't tell what it is. "I kind of feel like it has a message for us," he says.

Sometimes I hate how Creigh says things out loud.

Marko's sitting in our sleeping space, hands planted on the floor, high out of his skull. I sit next to him. I pretend I'm high too. His skin is turning the color of concrete. The warehouse ceiling rises three stories above us.

"It's like a cathedral," I tell Marko.

"It's an old Walmart," he says. "You're full of shit."

"I mean, the space inside is like the space inside a cathedral. It's so big."

I don't add, and all those people clutching shopping carts, wasn't that a kind of prayer?

"You can't have the space inside a cathedral without the cathedral, idiot." Marko tilts away from me. "You can't just compare one volume of air to another volume of air."

I always forget how pills turn him aggressively rational. "What would you know about cathedrals anyway, Friday? Cathedral would've just sunk your island faster."

He shakes his heavy head, keeps shaking like he forgot to stop. "Home didn't need a cathedral." He speaks like he's watching birds take flight. "Didn't need any fucking cathedral. You have no idea."

People come to look at the thing. Some girls no one likes. A mom and dad and three kids, dressed like they must have divvied up the same 5-pack of undershirts. The kids lay their shitty limbless action figures in the pool. "In case it wants to play." Kids who live here have more shitty limbless action figures than they could ever want.

One of the girls dangles a necklace over the water on a limp wrist. It's made all of feathers and faux old coins. She smiles nervously as she drops it, watches it settle under the water with wide eyes like it's a thousand fathoms away.

"—not a sea creature!" Marko is saying to someone. "Why would we keep that around?"

I walk over and he turns to me. He turns to everyone. "Doesn't it bother you? Eels wiggling around the bathroom where you learned to piss in a pot? Bigass crabs on the sofa where Pilar let you touch her tits the first time?"

No one meets his eyes.

An older woman and her husband kneel by the pool. She's holding a souvenir mug with *Sunny Key West!* emblazoned on its side. She sinks the mug into the water, dips up a cupful, pours it over the thing's back. The water unfurls in a glassy ribbon, sluices over and makes the thing shine.

Marko stands watch over the people drifting in and out, his body hunched in a shape I recognize from somewhere. The man and woman take turns pouring. When they go they leave the mug behind. Marko crosses his arms, sets his feet wide, watches them leave. I realize he looks like my dad.

Someone mentions that there's a woman out front looking for day laborers so I go outside. There's no one there.

I feel an ache to go back to the thing, which seems weird so I resist. Instead I lean against the wall of the warehouse. Big plastic letters are tacked up on the wall. They used to say something more but all that's left is MART. Someone added words with yellow spray paint so now it says, Saint MART's Home for Flooded Children. Back when this was a store, the letters would glow at night. If I were standing here then, I'd be bathed in light.

Creigh comes out waving the secretary like a surrender flag. No signal, no signal. I've seen commercials where they take people a mile underground and their secretaries still plug them into the world. Not in Saint Mart's.

"Ugh." Creigh folds the secretary into an airplane. "Wanna go fly it off the roof?"

On the roof we sit with our legs over the edge. Creigh's knees are scabbed like a kid's. The secretary sails on the breeze for a moment, creased screen flickering. Then it takes a nosedive and crashes into the parking lot.

For a while we stare at the tiny dot of it on the pavement and don't say anything. I bite my lip.

"I couldn't wait to get out of Norfolk," I tell Creigh. "You're not supposed to miss places you couldn't wait to get out of." I hold up my bandaged hand. "This? It wasn't cause I saw some dude hitting on Cheyenne. She's trash. I don't even care anymore."

Creigh feeds the silence. I'm surprised he doesn't ask what the real reason was, and then I'm angry at myself for wanting him to ask, and then I try to let it pass but the words bust out. "I went by this building. With a sign. It looked like, I don't know, it looked like this dance studio where my little sister took ballet. That was it. So I punched it. The wall. Really hard."

The silence grows and grows. There's a breeze. There's a sunset so chemical and resplendent it's hard to look at. My ass starts to hurt from sitting on gravel. "She wasn't even good." I don't know why I add this. "My sister. She sucked at ballet."

More silence, and all of a sudden I get up and take the stairs really fast, because I have this feeling that Creigh is crying and I don't want to look and find out.

I walk straight to the back of the store where the wading pool is. The people have drifted away. I think the thing is alone, but coming around the partition I hit Marko. He looks like I caught him with his dick out.

He swallows and says, "It keeps getting stiller."

There are times when I can feel water rising through my skull, lapping at the top of my brain. Until I take a deep breath I'm not sure that my throat isn't clogged with brine.

"Hey, Marko," I say. "How about you prove to me that magic is real."

He smells like Natty Ice. "Fine." He sighs. "How about, you tell me the name of my island, I'll give you all the magic in the world. Hell, I'll give you the first spells the wind gods used to sing land up from water."

I clench my teeth. I look at the floor. I kick the partition shelf and it clangs so that someone yells at me to quiet the fuck down.

"Huh, Asa? What's the name of my island?"

I glance at the wading pool, but it's so dark I can't see the thing. Probably it couldn't give me an answer anyway. Marko sighs and walks away.

Creigh pokes me awake the next morning. His fingernails are so bitten they leave blood on my sleeve. "The thing," he says. He looks at me but not at me. "I think it's dead."

I walk with him to the wading pool. The thing has curled itself on the towel. It's shrunk down to a quarter of its former size, skin wrinkled and split like chapped lips. The face is unchanged, same sickened grimace only now in miniature. It's kind of crusty. A great cloud of mucus has oozed out of it, soaked the towel, slicked the water surface with iridescence. Swirls of purple, turquoise, gold. Marko plunges his hand into the water, retrieves his Trudy Keane novel. His arm comes out sheathed in rainbows.

I poke the thing. It's like poking a dried apple. I wonder if it will start to smell. I wonder if I should call my sister and tell her how beautiful she was when she danced.

"We should bury it," says Creigh.

"My book," says Marko. "Fucking weirdo ruined my book."

. . . .

We take it out to the strip of dirt behind the warehouse. There's a chain-link fence separating the parking lot from the highway, and shrimpy trees and vines and stuff hug the wire. We pick a spot under some honeysuckle.

Creigh goes at the dirt with a pickaxe as long as he is, flailing so hard I can see the muscles of his back through his T-shirt. He looks animal and full of rage. I'm scared to interrupt him so the hole gets bigger and bigger, way bigger than the shrunken thing needs.

I hold it against my chest, wrapped in a pillowcase. I'm holding a husk. Everything that gave it weight and substance has run out in a thin layer, dispersed by the water. I lower it into the pit.

We stare down into the hole and I ask if anyone wants to say anything.

Marko tosses the book in, shrugging. "Shit was ruined anyway."

Creigh looks like the only words he wants to say are in languages lost to him.

We pack dirt into the hole and stamp it down. Marko goes inside. I kind of think Marko's on those pills too much, and I wonder if I should say something to him. Maybe tomorrow.

Things aren't going to change. We aren't going to get jobs. Animals aren't going to pad through our dreams and whisper the answers. The sea will keep creeping. The Earth will grow smaller and shiver in its sleep.

Creigh works his fingers into the chain link and rattles it so honeysuckle leaves leap off and flutter to the ground. Sometimes Creigh surprises me.

"It was stupid anyway," he says.

"You don't know that. It could have been some kind of extraterrestrial genius. It could have been the second coming of the goddamn Messiah."

"No." Creigh invents an alphabet in the dirt with his shoe. "No. I mean. It was stupid to think we could save it."

Sweetheart

Paxton is your baby boy, born just after you got out of the army, your peacetime child. He turned six last month but already he's got a sweetheart who lives next door. He makes her crowns out of dandelions and shares his Fruit-Blaster cups with her. She brings him marbles that hum and lets him position her antennae into funny shapes. He has a lisp that the speech therapist has given up on, and she has clicking mandibles, but in their invented language of coos and giggles they are both poets. They sit out in the yard and very seriously lay grass on each other's arms, and the sunlight cocoons them.

You and Denise watch them through the kitchen window. Denise is an old army buddy and she gets it. All of it.

You say something like, No surprise he's got a sweetheart already. Just look at his daddy.

Denise laughs rough and loud. Regular little Casanova, isn't he? Regular little intergalactic Casanova. Damn. And I can't even get a date.

You want to date an ET?

She shudders. Lord, girl, don't joke. Then she bites her lip. Nothing against Pax, of course. It's super cute.

You nod. They're just babies, I figure. Sweetheart's a good thing to have. And he's a good kid.

She agrees with you and pours the dregs of the margarita pitcher into your glass.

You take Paxton and Sweetheart to the water park and lie in a chaise while they jump off the foam pirate ship. Only ten minutes before Pax runs up sobbing.

She won't come up! I yelled and I yelled, but she won't!

You fly to the edge of the pool, terrified the little alien has drowned on your watch, but then you realize she has gills.

Paxton crouches next to you, wiping his nose. Come up, stu-pid, he shouts at the water. Stupid stupid *stu-pid.*

Don't say stupid, Pax. Hush. She's okay.

You buy them hot dogs and try not to be disgusted when Sweetheart pincers hers into bits and tucks them into pouches on her sides. Pax trumps her by mashing his entire dog into his cheeks and opening his mouth to display it.

They whisper to each other the whole bus ride home. You realize you don't even know if Sweetheart is a girl.

. . . .

At night with his voice full of sleep Pax asks you what love is, and you spin out some bullshit about caring for someone very very much. He gets serious in the dark.

Okay, so then, I think I love Sweetheart.

You don't want him to hear so you mouth the word, Congratulations.

Things start to change. On the radio, on TV. Human Pride is a big deal with advertisers. Coke does a whole, *One People One Planet* campaign. The pundits start asking why so much tax money still goes to the army. It's been years since there was a conflict, hasn't it? And don't we all know where the real threat is? Their voices purr hungrily and their eyes flicker toward the sky.

You don't think Paxton would get what *Strategic Containment and Deportation* means, but you hide the newspaper headlines from him anyway.

Jesus, says Denise, it's happening. Just like that. We spent all that time kicking in doors and we could have just said, look over there, look at the ones with the tentacles! She wipes her mouth with the back of her hand. And I know the ones next door seem okay, but I mean, really. You know?

You do know.

One night the authorities come banging on Sweetheart's door. Some of the neighbors go out in the street to watch but you take Paxton into your bedroom and turn the cartoons up loud. He falls asleep with his head on your stomach. In the morning you say, What the heck, huh. Let's take a day off school.

It works until six that evening when he gets two Italian ices out of the freezer and says, I'm going over to Sweetheart's.

Why don't you stay in with me tonight? You try to say it nonchalantly but he catches on. His chin starts to shake.

I'm *going* over to *Sweetheart's*.

Aliens are in some trouble right now, okay? It's not safe for you.

Is Sweetheart safe?

Something about his look makes you feel guilty, and feeling guilty gets you a little pissed. Look. Sweetheart went away for a while. You can make some new friends, how about. You want to go over to Shira Allen's? Shira Allen just got a trampoline.

Pax makes a wordless noise and flies to the front door, but it's locked and with an Italian ice in each hand he's stuck. He flings himself against the window and leaves snot prints on the glass.

Without knowing where the words come from you're telling him, You'll understand when you're older. He stiffens and turns, tear-bright eyes spearing through you. I don't understand *now*, he screams. His voice so full of rage it's like music. *I don't understand now.*

He flings an Italian ice at you, and melting strawberry sucrose bursts across your chest.

Love explodes in you, how smart he is, how he was once a part of you but is no longer. You step up so close that the red syrup on your shirtfront smears on him as well. You get in your room this minute, you hiss. You *never* talk to me that way again.

He slams his door but doesn't get it quite right and opens it and slams it again. He's going to hate you for a couple of days, that's okay. Hate is nothing; you've known love. It stampedes through your veins. You could tell him about it. You could tell him you had sweethearts, you had cocoons of sunlight too. You could tell him about his father. You could tell him about the long nights in Delta Company, the dreams and the grit that never came out from under your eyelids. But you won't.

In the silent hallway you stare at his closed door. You'd understand if Pax never trusted you again, but also you know he will. He will dry his eyes and open the door. He will take Shira Allen to school dances and eat waffle fries with his friends and make JV football. He will hear talk on the radio of uniting against the alien menace and change it to Top 40 without thinking. Once in a while, he'll remember Sweetheart and freeze on the sidewalk. Then after a moment he'll shake his head and keep walking, a song he can't place running through his head, the sun heavy and warm on his limbs.

I'm Sorry Your Daughter Got Eaten by a Cougar

Old man Windson sends me up the mountain with a wagonful of food for Mr. and Mrs. Drake. He tells me that they have not been in his grocery since it happened. He also tells me that last time they were in, they did not stock up on nearly enough basic items to carry them through the past three weeks.

The weight of canned corn and two sides of bacon and rice and flour and a bushel of peaches has me sweating by the time I make it to their house. I stand on their porch and huff and hope they will not resent my mothering. I know I should not presume, I know I have never been anywhere near where they are now, but I also know that everyone must eat. Everyone must have the strength to continue.

They let me in. "Bless you, Pickle," they say. "You and old man Windson both." I follow Mrs. Drake from the porch, down the hallway into the kitchen. She moves as though she is afraid of waking something huge. Mr. Drake unloads the wagon of food. We sip tap water in silence, though a couple of times Mrs. Drake opens and shuts her mouth. The only words that make it out are more thank you's. I wonder if perhaps she cannot say anything else. Maybe once you lose something so big, there is no point in holding on to little things like speech. Who needs it? What could it possibly do?

As I'm walking out, I notice a door off the hallway that is slightly ajar. Inside, there's a long clothesline piled on the rag-rug, with clothes still clothespinned onto it. Little pink sweaters and polka-dotted skirts. Socks that would fit on my thumbs. A knitted hat with teddy-bear ears.

The thunderstorms this year have been unpredictable. I imagine the Drakes standing on their porch, paralyzed with indecision. Do we leave the clothes out there to get drenched? Do we admit that it doesn't matter? Or do we go out and take them down, touch them with our own hands for the very last time, because there's not—there's never going to be—

Carrying the whole clothesline in must have been a compromise. They didn't have to touch a thing.

Some nights when I cannot sleep, I close my eyes and watch the cougar stalk the dark country of my eyelids. The cat is as big as the shuttle Davy drives. Its eyes glow gold and turquoise and green and a hundred other colors that exist nowhere else. Its front paws are human hands, and it is wearing bracelets. When it opens its mouth I see Phoebe Drake curled in its gullet, sound asleep.

. . . .

I don't mind playing delivery girl for old man Windson. With the valley so sparse, you snatch on any excuse for human interaction. I pass the Drakes' drive every day I head into town. Their place has the same feel as mine—both tiny houses, nestled back against the mountain, the huge quiet of the black rock and hemlock needles bearing down.

Except to be technical, I shouldn't call it "my place." Davy might take exception to that, if he ever got wind of it. It's unlikely, though. Eleven months out of the year he's eleven hundred miles away.

Davy Drum. My wedding veil had not been in the closet for six months when he heard the call of the shuttling life and lit on out of town. It's been five years since we lived together as man and wife.

The first week he was gone I made a list of qualities I would no longer tolerate in a man. One of them was Never Comes Around, and another one was Pees in Bottles While Driving, and since then our relationship has been pretty much moot.

It works out okay. When Davy comes through town he crashes with friends, and I get to play both "house" and "independent woman," as long as I don't press for alimony. To be honest, if I could go back to my high-school self, waving my pom-poms and hollering as Davy ploughs the ball into the end zone, well, I might give some advice to certain people. I might burst a rosy bubble or two. But, you know. I can't.

. . . .

Mr. and Mrs. Drake are in old man Windson's grocery, meandering down the produce aisle. It's good to see them—I've been worried. They come up to me and say hello. I can't help but wonder if they have some sort of vitamin deficiency. Their eyes have a yellowish tint. It gives me the shivers. My first thought is that something is terribly wrong. That's not how it's supposed to be at all. But it occurs to me that I have no idea how it's supposed to be. Maybe when you're grieving, your eyes are supposed to turn golden and glassy. Maybe all those with cloven hearts forget basic things, like the layout of their local grocery. Maybe when Mr. Drake clutched my arm and said, "Pickle, where is the meat cooler? We've been wandering around this store for an hour, please, where has it gone?" maybe his hands were supposed to feel cold and scaly.

And maybe those who encounter the grief-stricken all react in the same way too. Maybe all of them sleepwalk through the rest of their day, stumble home, get halfway through making a pot of tea and collapse on the linoleum, pressed up against the dishwasher, not crying but not really breathing either, trying to accustom themselves to the devouring hole that has opened up in their chests. That's just how it goes. Right?

When old man Windson doesn't need me for errands I wait tables in Eddie Squeak's bar. Mostly it's a watering hole for shuttlers passing through the valley, but we've got a decent cast of locals to round the place out. The mood since the cougar attack has been tense. The whole valley sleeps with one eye open.

Mae Woods and her husband, Clovis, are in tonight, squaring off on either side of a booth.

"We're getting the hell out of here," Mae tells me. "This ain't a place to raise children. This valley sold its soul to the devil. I've been saying it for years, and this mess with the Drakes is the last straw. We're hightailing for the suburbs."

I replace their empty beer pitcher. Clovis looks up at me with dog-tired eyes. "What we are doing," he enunciates, "is evaluating our prospects in a rational and level-headed manner."

"My sister's got a condo next to hers that's up for rent. Little patch of lawn in front of every one. Perfect for a picnic supper. Can you imagine trying for a picnic supper in this valley? Forget cougars, the kiddies would wind up impaled on those awful black rocks."

Mae was a year below me in high school. I can still feel the homecoming tiara in my fingers as I lifted it off my own head and set it on hers.

"Each condo's got one cute maple tree inside a fence," she says. "That's what I call family friendly. All these pine trees give me the willies."

They're hemlocks, I want to tell her. Clovis asks could he please get some ketchup.

"And this *rain*," I hear Mae say as I walk away. "Good Lord, I can't stand this rain."

It has been raining a lot. But let's be clear, at the moment she says that, the storm has broken, the clouds are parting, and if you look out the window the whole parking lot is bathed in moonlight.

The dead man shows up at my house that night. It's been three weeks since he last came around so at first I don't let him in. If you think I am just going to twiddle my thumbs and wait for the mood to strike you, you have got another thing coming, mister, I tell him. I didn't put up with that from Davy, I will not put up with it from you, understand?

"I'm deeply sorry." The dead man spreads his hands before him. His eyes are wide. "Pickle, you must believe me. There were matters that required my attention."

How can I resist? He is so contrite, and so handsome. How can a man stay so handsome when he's been dead two hundred years? He was a soldier in the war, shot through the chest by a man he had trusted as a brother. He told me this to explain why I didn't have to worry, he would always be faithful. I understand the pain of disloyalty, he declared, kissing my hair. I have never been able to help myself when it comes to men, especially men in uniform. Even when I can tell they mean trouble.

We sit on the lumpy futon and he rubs my feet.

"You shouldn't have gone away," I admonish. "Who knows what could have happened to me. Did you hear about the little girl? All they found was one of her feet. How would you feel if the next time you showed up, all that was left was one of my feet?"

He bends around and kisses my toes. "I would be surprised, dearest, that the foul beast had deigned to relinquish such a choice piece of flesh."

I could kick him in the face but I don't. Who knows, his head might fall off and maggots might pour out of his body. I sometimes have a feeling that if I clutch him too hard or wrap my legs too wildly around his waist, he will collapse like he is carved out of dust. I've never figured out exactly what he is, or why he chose to come to me. Is he a ghost? No, there is heat under his flesh. Is he a zombie? No, he doesn't smell like death.

Part of me envies Mr. and Mrs. Drake. They are both whole living breathing people who interact with each other on a daily basis. In high school I anticipated a life like that. But I am no good at taking action. Like now for instance. What I should really do is just say, here's the deal, dead soldier, no more sex until you tell me straight, are you a zombie or a ghost or what? But for some reason whenever he shows up the question goes clean out of my head.

Every so often I get dressed for work, I get my purse, I leave the house—but then instead of walking down the road I climb up the mountain. I can't control it, or predict it, or explain it. I get out of breath pretty quickly; the mountain is steep. Where the rocks are bare they are slippery, and where they are covered the detritus conceals crevasses and loose scree.

I lie down on the ground. The rocks have heartbeats. They throb fast and irregular and infect me with their fear. When the wind blows, the whole bulk of the mountain chain shivers and the trees whine. I don't know what to do with such a big scared thing. Sometimes I hum parts of Lance Harbinger's greatest hits but that doesn't help much. I am no good at remembering songs.

Lying on the ground, I stuff my mouth full of pine needles. They taste sour and rotten and they teach me new kinds of yearnings. The yearning to decay. The yearning to collapse, to finally let go. They prick my throat, my tongue, my lips, and when I finally spit them out the ground is tinged pink with mouth blood.

I have to be careful to brush all the dirt and needles off me before I walk down to the valley. Otherwise old man Windson will shout to me, "Who have you been rolling around with, girlie?" and try to sweep me off with his long-handled broom.

Eddie Squeak is not bartending very well tonight. He has something on his mind. His grandmother just died and he received a package from her estate in the mail. It's a tiny locked box.

"The hell am I supposed to do?" Squeak looks a little frantic. "Ain't no keyhole. And no hinges either. How'm I supposed to open a box with no hinges?"

He leans against the bar and does not provide refills and doesn't seem troubled when patrons leave fuck-yous instead of tips. I call Cristoff in to check on him. Cristoff is the bouncer.

"She had a fortune," Squeak tells us. "You got no idea. She slept on the sheets of the empress of China. She bribed gravity to let her house alone. And it's in here. I know it. She wouldn't have left it to anybody else."

He clutches the object in both hands and drops his head between his arms. Cristoff's stony features rearrange themselves into an expression of concern. He looks at what Squeak is holding.

"All due respect?" Cristoff says. "That's a chicken egg."

It does look a lot like a chicken egg. But Squeak will not listen. In an icy voice he reminds Cristoff that he is paying him to deter unsavories from entering, not laze around the bar and insult Squeak's deceased family. Cristoff stalks away and Squeak turns to me. "I'm sorry, Pickle." His mouth quavers. "Something's happening to me. First the Drake girl, now Grandma? There's death in the air. I can feel it."

I assure him I feel it too. When I finally get off work at two in the morning I pass him sitting on the curb. There are tears on his face. He is holding the white ovoid treasure chest up to the moon, begging it to give up its secrets.

In high-school cheerleading my favorite move was the seven quarter cradle. The base girls would put their hands under my feet, lock into a full extension, I would go tight, and they would shoot me up, up, up. I'd tuck my body in and do two forward flips and for a moment at the apex, I was nothing. I had no body. There was no up or down or past or future or ground or sky. Then I'd straighten out into a pike pose and drop into the arms of the base girls and they would catch me gentle as a baby bunting.

Davy said the seven quarter cradle was his favorite too, because when I flipped over he could see my panties. He told me that the night he proposed. "You know, babe, that thing you used to do? Your legs up in the air like that? Well, first time I seen that? That's when I fell in love."

I get a piece of mail addressed to the Drakes. Normally I'd just put it back out for the mailman but I want a reason to check on them. The wood of their porch is rotting through. My foot goes through the top step and I catch myself on the railing. The house is dark. I'm almost convinced no one is home when suddenly Mr. Drake appears, beckoning me through the door, leading me down the hallway as silent as falling hemlock needles.

It's hard to tell in the gloom but I don't think he looks any better. His eyes are still yellow and he walks hunched over. He could use a shave. Mrs. Drake comes into the room and it's hard not to jump, because she is very successfully cultivating a unibrow. She used to babysit for me sometimes. She's the one who taught me how to put on eyeliner.

They say things like, "Thanks so much, Pickle," and "Darn postman!" and "You've been so kind these past weeks." They bob weirdly up and down, their knees always bent, their backs never straight. Mr. Drake's hands are on his wife's shoulders, then her waist. She touches his jawline, his chest. They never lose contact with each other.

I say thank you, no trouble, really, and then there's an awkward silence. Their sink is filled with brown water. The faucet drips into it. Plink. Plink.

They walk me down the hallway. The door to the room with the clothesline is shut. There are dark stains around the door knob.

When I go to shut the front door behind me the hinges rip out of the wall—the wood is soft as tofu!—and the whole thing falls on top of me. I stagger out from underneath and it collapses on the porch. Paint flakes and rotting splinters pepper my blouse.

Mrs. Drake gasps, "Oh, goodness!" and Mr. Drake chuckles, "Nice catch, Pickle." Neither of them moves to pick up the door.

We get a whole bunch of shuttlemen in the bar that night. The vestibule is full of rain-soaked shuttlesuits and helmets. The room smells like wet mustaches. At first all they can do is complain about the storm, but then someone mentions Phoebe Drake. There is no talk of the parents, only the cougar. The shuttlemen were not aware that cougars still prowled these mountains. They are outraged. Arguments start up over how best to slaughter it.

"Smother the mountain with poison gas!" declares one. "Fill the woods with remote-control assassins!" shouts another.

"Now guys," says Cristoff. "Let's not get out of hand. It's just one cougar, after all."

This catches my attention. I look up at Cristoff but his arms are crossed and his face looks just as much like a double-bolted freezer door as ever. The shuttlemen fall over themselves in their hurry to disagree. The ones furthest along in their drinking fall over literally. How dare he say "just one cougar"! One cougar with a taste for manflesh—for little girlflesh, no less. It's a threat to the security of the good people of this here valley. It's a threat to the dominion of good people everywhere!

The shuttlemen are experts at dominion. The shuttlemen's union is lobbying for a highway to be built from the Earth to Mars. How disgruntled these shuttlemen must be, stuck shuttling goods through a dark and rainy valley across the lonely surface of the Earth.

The dead man doesn't come around nearly enough and I am no good at keeping the emptiness of the house in check. The rain drums and drums. The best I can do is put my Lance Harbinger cassettes into the tape player and crank up the volume. The DJ at my prom played four Lance Harbinger songs, more than any other band. One was a slow song, but at that point

Davy had gone down to the moat to funnel a Budweiser with his friends. But he came back for the last song of the night, which was "Jump, Lele," the one that kept Lance at the top of the charts for six straight weeks. He implored us all:

Jump, Lele, baby
Jump with me tonight
Jump through to morning
We'll make it all right

And so we jumped. Everyone. It almost felt like we hadn't jumped, like instead the floor of the gymnasium fell out from under us. My ex-best-friend Janet and One-Legged Cordelia held my hands, and I could feel Davy's breath warm on the back of my neck. We were screaming out the words. The disco ball scattered stars over our faces. We rose into the air.

As the bar is closing up I go talk to Cristoff. I'm not sure how to say what I want to say. He looks as though he were hewn out of a great pillar of black rock. I pretend I'm talking to the mountain behind my house. That makes it easier.

"I can't get Phoebe Drake out of my head," I tell him. He raises his eyebrows and nods.

"I know."

He knows! I feel braver. "But I've got this awful feeling. I don't know who to tell. I'm ashamed."

"Ashamed of what?" The great pillar looks concerned.

"I—well—sort of—uh," but there's no way to get around it now. I have to spit out this viper coiling around my insides, and I have to spit it out to Cristoff. "Sometimes I—do you ever—feel relieved?"

"Relieved?" His eyes grow wide. "Yes, Pickle. I do."

The pillar turns kind! I venture to discover the precise nature of my viper. "It's like . . . who knew there were cougars left around here?"

"Exactly!" Cristoff thumps one fist against the wall with satisfaction. "No one expected it! We were all sinfully complacent. I've got a wife and three babies, did you know that, Pickle? And so of course my heart breaks for Mr. and Mrs. Drake. Of course. But when I think it could have been my own . . ." He shakes his head. "It's a sinful feeling, Pickle, it truly is. But I am relieved. Relieved that when the wake-up call came, it spared the ones I loved."

No. This isn't my viper at all. My viper has a subtler venom. I say good night to Cristoff then, because I am suddenly afraid of what he might find out.

The rain turns into hail as I walk home. Even the thick blanket of hemlock branches cannot shield the road from hailstones big as mouse skulls. I'm passing by the Drake's drive right then so I dodge up it. Maybe I can hang out in their house until the storm passes.

They haven't replaced the door. The porch is about to fall off the house and hailstones bounce over the threshold into the hallway. I let myself in. It doesn't seem like they're home. Windows are shattered and green vines peek into the living room. The room with that clothesline no longer has a door. Inside it is a mountain of sticks and leaves. It looks like a huge bird's nest. The clothesline and all of Phoebe's clothes have been woven among the sticks. There are dark clumps jammed into the gaps. I lean into the room and squint. Hair. The dark clumps are hair.

Something small and dense unfurls pain in my head. Hailstones. There's a hole gaping in the roof. I glance up and see white hailstones dropping out of the black, like I'm flying through space with stars speeding by.

I duck back into the hallway to avoid the hail. It roars inside and outside the house, but behind the roar I hear a noise. A creak, a keen—there is something in the kitchen. A faint clatter—a dark shape flashes across the hall. I take a step down the hallway. None of the lights work. The linoleum floor has peeled away and under my feet there is only glue and grime and cracking wood. The scrabbling grows louder. And then the shadows in the kitchen coalesce and bound down the hallway toward me. It is Mrs. Drake. Her hair is a mat that hangs down her back. She lopes with her hands grazing the floor.

I leap away and trip and stagger out to the porch. Mrs. Drake skids to a stop in the doorway. There is blood on her mouth. Her upper arms have teeth marks in them, and shreds of skin hang down to her elbows like fringe. I run out into the driveway but something makes me stop and turn around. Mr. Drake has joined her in the doorway. The beard he was growing is gone; instead his jaw is covered with oozing scabs. He wears one of Phoebe's tiny sweaters on his head. The Drakes paw at each other. They flail their arms at me and keen deep in their throats. I flee down the road and the hail pelts my arms and the next morning I am dotted all over with little round bruises.

. . . .

This valley sees very little of unrelenting grief. How was I supposed to know? How was anyone supposed to understand? We went to the memorial service and then went on with our lives.

The shuttlemen spend one evening in Squeak's, but next evening finds them in Morocco or California or the asteroid belt. They cannot really comprehend those of us who remain within the mountains. They cannot be blamed for that.

The dead man says, "Does this satisfy you? I am here. And I have brought you a picnic supper." But I'm not hungry and I'm not horny and I sort of wish he would leave. I bolt the door and yell through the window, "It's amazing how you can talk so fancy and still be such an insensitive *jerk*." But when I walk into the bedroom he's lying on the bed. I scream and run into the bathroom. He says, "Pickle, dearest, I beg you, listen!" and flings out an arm to stop me from slamming the door. I slam it anyway and sever his wrist. His hand falls onto the bathroom floor and skitters across the tile, groping for my feet. Through the door I hear him moan softly in pain. "Pickle. Help me."

Trying to move silently, I climb on top of the toilet and hug my knees against my chest. I squeeze my eyes shut very tightly and recite: *feet together, ex-tend, left arm, right arm, tuck, pop!* over and over again in my head. Eventually I hear him sigh. His hand scrabbles back under the bathroom door. When I'm sure he's gone, I sag off the toilet. I just manage to get the lid up in time before I'm retching, puking up everything in my stomach, heaving so hard I think I might flip inside out. Mae? Janet? Mrs. Drake? Can anyone tell me what this means?

. . . .

In Squeak's bar, the TV says there's been a shuttle collision. Everyone rushes outside to watch the sky. What they say is, one shuttle on a routine atmospheric trip ran head on into another one coming out of a time warp. "Cougars and time warps." Cristoff nudges me, grinning. "Who knew?"

The newswoman lists off the casualties. The name that catches my attention is David Drum.

Oh.

According to the crowd outside, the time warp has caught the shuttles in some kind of loop. They collide and explode and a peach blossom ignites in the sky. The flower falls a little ways, begins to flicker, until very abruptly it is snuffed out, and the collision reappears higher in the sky.

Holy shit, the shuttlemen say. Who'da thunk. Lookee there. But I don't really feel like looking at all. Estranged or no, I've got no desire to watch my husband, my high-school sweetheart, bloom and die over and over and over again.

Feeling their mortality, the shuttlemen tip well. I walk home with forty dollars in my pocket. The rain is giving the valley a rare reprieve and the sky floods with pink and gold. On the gravel road where no one can see me, I skip. I kick up stones and send them skittering into the bushes.

Something has lifted off my heart. It makes me want to do beautiful things. It makes me want to check up on the Drakes, one more time.

Their roof is completely gone. The walls have fallen away and lie mouldering in the earth. Whatever gestated in that house has finally sloughed off its cocoon of plywood and sheetrock.

The Drakes are still there, though. In what was once the living room, on what was once the couch but is now a mound of fibers and leaves. They are naked, bodies cupped, having marital relations out for everyone to see. His hands clutch her breasts, and the muscles of his back ripple, gleaming in the orange light of the sunset. She throws her head back, mouth open, teeth bared, exultation painted across her face.

In the driveway I tremble. For some reason I flash back to junior year, when my ex-best-friend Janet spent several weeks believing she could become a veterinarian. She read to me from her animal books, wide-eyed, giggling, *The penis of the male cat is covered by large, pointed, horny spines, or "papillae."* My body is shot through with heat, lines of fire that race from my chest to my groin.

They both freeze and stare at me. Did I make a noise? I didn't realize. For a moment everything is silent. I am held in their golden eyes. Then they leap up with a wild noise, flinging their heads around, clutching each other's hands. They scream at me.

Their screams pluck a note that first sounded when I was six and I lost my mother in a crowd. It sounded when Janet declared she was no longer my best friend, and when the tri-state cheerleading trophy went to a squad in the next valley. It sounded the night Davy left. But there are other notes playing as well in the raw and unchained throats of Mr. and Mrs. Drake. And the music is not sadness or anger or defiance or pain or anything else I will ever know. They no longer beckon to me. I will be left behind.

Far up the mountain I hear something else. Other screams from other voices. Other creatures calling to Mr. and Mrs. Drake.

They watch me for one last moment. It's okay, I whisper to them. Go. They turn and leap over the collapsed walls of their house, gallop up the mountain and disappear into the deep woods.

As I walk back to my house the rain begins again but I do not feel it. The mountain air enrobes me like a force field. Rays of light extend from my body out into the void. I imagine what it is like to give yourself over to pain. To become that porous. To have the mountain seep in everywhere. To wake up one morning and find your lungs replaced by two surging hemlock saplings. Your brain turned into a black stone covered with jewel-bright moss. Your dick transformed into the barbed apparatus of a mountain devil.

I am too full, I will burst. So I laugh. HA! The mountain thrums at the frequencies of my laughter. The trees ring like a thousand bells.

Then I break up with the dead man. I chase him out of the house with a knife. His eyes are liquid with fear, not for himself but for me. "Pickle, please!" He speaks like I am a spooked horse. "I love you!"

Love, ha. As if. He has no heart. To prove this I stab him in the chest. He does not explode or collapse or blow away on the wind. His lips form a wordless cry of pain and his eyes well up. A single maggot wriggles out of the wound and drops into the wet grass.

I tell him, "I don't want to see you here anymore. Get back under the ground. You have no place in this world. I have no place for you."

Rain plasters his hair to his head. He extends an arm to me. What a fine arm it is; muscles neatly toned, nails clean and trim.

But I keep my face expressionless and stand with my arms crossed until finally his shoulders sag, and he turns and leaves. My eyes follow him down the mountain until he has disappeared from view. Even then I don't cry.

It seems cruel, doesn't it? But I had to do this.

I had to do this because I am pregnant.

The dead man is the father. We used protection, sure, but early on I noticed that the used condoms all had smoking holes blasted through the ends of them. Since then I've had a feeling this might happen. And no baby of mine will be born into a house filled with residues of gravedust and melancholy.

I will have a daughter. I will name her Lele, after the girl in Lance Harbinger's number-one single, because honestly that is the most sublime music I have ever heard. I will explain to her that her father was a liar and a traitor, who betrayed his comrades-in-arms and so was executed by them. Together we will come to forgive him.

I will take her out into the night when it's raining. I will hold her up into the sky just like she's about to do her own seven quarter cradle. "Lookee there!" I will yell, and thunder will crash and lightning will split the sky into a thousand feline grins.

Don't say I'm nuts or anything. I'm not. I know this will make baby Lele cry. For each of her wails, I will wail louder. She will howl and I will scream. We'll rend the air so terribly that the rain will be afraid to fall on us. The raindrops will stare at us as they go by.

If our lungs are strong enough our wails will carry up the mountaintops and the untamed things will pause. If we are lucky, Mr. and Mrs. Drake will prick their ears. They will remember the long-ago day when they blessed me and called me kind. We will pull them down the mountain, and the cougar too, and all of the windswept creatures with bright fangs and brighter eyes. All around us, behind curtains of rain, beasts will cavort and moan and tumble. My lawn will be churned into a black swamp. The mud will splash up on my calves as I leap up, to bring Lele closer to the sky.

That is how I will let her know. That is how I will tell her, my perfect child, just how far I would go for her. Because the truth is, there is nothing the Drakes did that I would not also do. We are all three human beings, after all. Maybe they would disagree, but I know better. I saw what they did and it is what humans do for each other. They tear the roofs off their houses. They peel bands of skin from their arms with their own teeth. They let themselves be penetrated by the giant thorny penises of wild cat-men. Because otherwise, what would we be? And what is love, anyway?

Later at night after I have laved the mud and rain and white flecks of animal spittle from Lele's face, I will lay her in the cradle. I will pull the quilt to her chin and tuck her in. I will hum to her a gentle version of the song that bears her name. I will listen to her hushed exhalations and feel my heart expand, until she and I are all that exists in this tiny valley, ringed by these black mountains, on this desperate planet, under the trembling stars. I will stand in the doorway until she has fallen asleep. I will not let her grow up in a world without fear.

Rich People

Nobody stopped me. I smiled at the doormen like we were old friends. I followed the other guests and walked like I knew exactly where I had to be. The hallways were dim and reddish. Sometimes I made wrong turns and had to double back; even then I walked surely. As I got farther into the house there were more people about, and a deep humming pervaded the air. Some guests had hooks embedded in their necks and shoulders that trailed long graceful streamers. The flickering sconces made everybody look like stained-glass saints.

Finally I reached the ballroom. Usually such places are a disappointment, but here the floor was a rink of gold. The walls soared up, the ceiling obscured by vapor and heat and candle smoke. Everywhere people stood and spoke to each other, their mouths bright clots of blood that slid around their faces. I moved through the crowd and caught flecks of conversation like insects in my hair.

"She's really opening herself up to the opportunity of this country," someone said.

"That submarine is just not a joy I want to live without any longer."

So this was the hum. It was as though they were putting on a show for me, though they were not. Even their most unguarded selves were a sumptuous performance. I felt awe.

Nearly every day I have passed by this house. I know its outside like a favorite picture book. The shards of glass embedded in the top of the garden wall, the gargoyles vomiting dirty water. I had always imagined what lay inside to be painted in colors that my eyes could not comprehend. Instead it felt as though I were descending deeper into my own brain. Anything I could think of existed somewhere in the ballroom. I saw a woman so laden with diamonds she had to bend over and crawl on all fours. The strands of diamonds hung down all around her body and over her head, making her look like a shaggy, sparkling dog.

A butler stepped into my vision, offering to squeeze truffle oil into my mouth from a dropper. I let it fall on my lips and then thought why the hell not; I kissed his meaty neck with reverence. Under his skin, his pulse deferred.

I rode a surge of blood or ocean. Imminently it would break upon the shore and I would learn something about myself. Seeking air I clicked across the golden floor, slipped through the glass doors and out onto the balcony. The night was sharp and alien. Many people mingled out here also, styling themselves explorers on a new planet. A woman lifted an ancient diving helmet off her head, shook out her long hair, and smiled to her companions. Behind the house a balcony jutted out several stories above the ground. I went to the edge and looked over the railing. Glittering below was a fountain, a wide expanse of water in which many fish the size of men, and a young boy, had been turned to stone and now pissed and spat water elegantly through the air. Beyond the fountain was a severely curated lawn. Beyond the lawn someone had practiced the art of creating fragrant wilderness, vines and weeping trees that trembled in the breeze with desire. Beyond the trees I could see the lights of the city and the place I had come from.

A knot of people next to me laughed dangerously. One young man held a knife in his palm. Everyone backed away from him, licking their lips. He pinched the spine of the blade between his thumb and forefinger and flung the knife high up into the night. It vanished into the darkness, and he was so rich—everyone was so rich—that it never came down.

Earlier that day I had decided it might be easier to talk about myself as though I were a separate person. For example:

Fuck that Suya, what a fucking pig! Would you get a load of the place she lives in? Hair and candy wrappers and disintegrating snot rags in the corners. She promised to vacuum this weekend, but when has Suya ever kept a promise? The counters and stove going gummy with dust and crumbs and thick grease.

There she is right now, curled on her ass in one corner of the futon. She digs an M&M out from a crease in the cushion and checks to make sure the old woman is not watching before she pops it into her mouth. Watch how her eyes close momentarily at the sweetness of the candy, as though it is the only brush with the sublime she can ever hope for.

The fan stirs dead skin cells around the air. Suya woke this morning with a dark room in her mind. She does not know either how to enter or close the door. She wonders if the old woman can detect her thoughts. She doubts it. This idea is both solace and intolerable to her. She swallows her candy-flavored saliva, and then her mouth is bare again.

A wail reminds her to rise and walk to the bathroom. White flecks of toothpaste spit coat the mirror like sea spray. Long dark hairs cling to the walls of the shower where Suya has pasted them. Pink scum rings the toilet bowl. The baby is strapped in its bouncy chair on the tile floor. It is coolest in the bathroom, and the baby's skin had been feeling hot to the touch.

When Suya sticks her head through the doorway the baby begins to bob and flap. White-tinged bubbles cluster in the corners of its mouth like amphibious eggs. The baby wails again and some of those bubbles slide down the creases of its chin, drip into the bib. Despite this Suya does not go to it. She stands at the threshold, the fingers of one hand resting barely on the doorframe, and she looks.

This is not Suya's baby. That is not Suya's mother. There is a fourth resident of this apartment, a man, the center around which they orbit. The crone is his mother. The baby is his child by a woman who loved him in the past. Suya loves him in the present. Because she is an idiot, whether he loves her in return is not a question she has asked. Yesterday morning he went out to pick up lozenges and made the choice not to return home. In the time since then he makes this same choice over and over.

In his absence, Suya feels the strands of fake motherhood, daughterhood, attempt to grow between herself, the crone, and the baby, like the filaments of an invasive and relentless algae. Revolted, she swipes at her shoulders. She tilts her head and tries to view the baby not as a being but a mark, a record, a proof. Once he cared for someone else as much/more than Suya, and he continues, in some way, to care for this person. Suya grooms her jealousy like she might enter it into a pageant. She tilts her head the other way and pictures the baby without any skin.

How rich were they? Here's how rich.

Rich enough that they could live forever and never be hurt by anything. Or else, rich enough that they could be hurt by everything and never need to worry. Some people there were even rich enough that they could slice off little bits of their own flesh and serve it to their friends on top of rice balls, like sushi. They nibbled each other, and then there were little gilt comment cards on which they rated their friends based on freshness and tenderness of flesh, superlative mouthfeel, choiceness of cut. I stood by the buffet tables and watched two young people descend into a quarrel over the poor ratings they had given each other. They rolled their eyes and sneered, their lips still flavorful with the fat of the other.

A tall man next to me laughed. "You see?" He rested the fingers of one hand on my elbow. "No friendship is so strong it cannot be destroyed by ratings."

I told him I didn't know what he meant at all. I asked him where were the foods that allowed you to forget everything in your life before the moment of biting down.

"That will take a long time," he said, and then he used some of his money to go talk to people more interesting than me.

At the other end of the buffet there was a table piled with whole roast chickens. Hundreds of them, bodies gleaming with crispy fat and smoke-infused salt and crackling herbs, stacked into a pyramid that towered over my head. The smell was nearly sexual.

There was an attendant nearby—who looked like every part of him was tucked into his pants—whose job was to ensure that when guests came to choose a chicken, they did not choose one from the bottom of the pyramid and cause all the rest to tumble down.

I went over to the table and the attendant helped me to select a hen from the top. "What will you name it?" he asked.

"Can I distinguish myself by refusing to give it a name?"

"No. Many people have already done that."

I named it Voltairine.

There were various pins you could affix to your chicken to make it unique. I chose two pins that looked like long-lashed eyes and stabbed them into my chicken's breast. People carried their chickens by inserting a fist into the body cavity and balancing it like a puppet on their arm. When they encountered another person with a chicken, they would both bobble the chickens around on their fists. They made different voices for their chickens, and had them converse about current events or philosophy or other scintillating subjects. Grease and herbs dripped from their elbows.

A woman who had been ironed flat nudged her chicken coyly against mine. She had affixed a pair of bright red lips and a rainbow flag to her chicken. "But how can we possibly be enjoying ourselves when other people elsewhere are so sad?" her chicken asked mine.

I was flooded with terror that I would be found out, but I summoned strength to quell it and forced my chicken to speak. "Impossible pleasure is the only kind I want."

Her chicken laughed. "How of the now!"

My chicken understood then that there was nothing she could say that would distinguish her from the rich chickens. There was no belief she could espouse more extreme than the beliefs they could adopt for fashion. My breath came more quickly and I tried to remember why I had come here. The woman raised her chicken to my lips. "Would you like?"

Per etiquette, I took a big bite from the thigh. I raised my chicken up and she took a bite in kind. The flesh was perfect, juicy, redolent with flavor. I ate more, trying to submerge my fear. We stood linked together in a circle, scraping with our teeth, ravenous, altered.

Suya dresses the crone. She combs the crone's hair into a ponytail at the back of her skull. It is a ponytail of corn silk. Suya holds it lightly in her fist. It would not be nearly strong enough to lift the crone from the ground.

Suya cleans the crone's face. She uses a washcloth to swab white residue from the creases of the crone's cheeks. With her fingertips she massages lotion into the crone's jowls. She colors the face with blush—Vintage Peach Blossom—and eye shadow—Intrepid Taupe—nothing garish.

The late morning sun is bleaching the curtains. Suya tries to find her reflection in the window, but her gaze slips beyond, over the city, past the apartment towers, to the rise of a verdant hill. What is Suya thinking here? Very little. Each of her motions feels like the result of a long mechanical process originating somewhere distant and inaccessible. She tries to imagine living in accord with her own will; it is like leaping across a canyon, and every time her mind falls short.

Suya fastens a necklace around the crone's neck. She arranges the glass gems against the crone's breast. She tucks a shawl around the crone's shoulders.

She trims the crone's fingernails. The crone's nails are like baby nails, thin and flexible, the milky-blue color of moonstone. Suya hews them mercilessly. The crone has a hangnail on her index finger. Suya seizes it with the nail clippers but jerks them too quickly. Instead of severing the hangnail, she pulls it up the old woman's arm, the way you might pull a string to open a bag of dog food. The old woman's papery skin is parted to her elbow. Suya gags and clamps the shawl over the crone's forearm. Blood seeps through the open weave.

The microwave dings. It is taquitos.

Suya swears and flies to the bedroom to find the crone a new shawl. The crone's closet is a tropical rain forest. Hibiscus-toned polyester. Tangerine viscose trimmed with bromeliad bows. Palm-frond prints, and leopard, and sequined parrots. Suya tears dresses from their hangers, hurls them across the floor, flings them over herself. She empties the closet until she collapses in a puddle of chemical fabrics. Get it together, Suya. Suya! Remember, even when you have nothing, you still have kindness.

The baby has been wailing this whole time. Its wails merge with the throbbing mechanical systems of the apartment complex. The walls are made of wailing, the ceiling, the floor. Suya stands in the kitchen and munches a soggy taquito. She licks grease from the web of her thumb. She sets the empty plate in the sink. She grips the edge of the counter very tightly with both hands, then she lets go.

. . . .

I don't know how people knew it was time to go outside. They swept me with them, down the grand staircase set with luminaries, out into the back garden. The fountain rippled in the moonlight. People thronged on the lawn. I swanned among them. Every part of me felt sated, dazed, and not only because I had eaten.

One of the things they enjoyed the most was slicing open the carcasses of animals and sliding inside them as though they were sleeping bags. On this beautiful half-moon of lawn, everybody was finally getting what they wanted. The man with the knife knelt in the grass and brought his blade through the belly of a dead tiger. His knife was a foot long and made of bone and it opened the tiger from throat to groin. His audience watched with eyes round enough to finally understand how good they had it. Her white belly fur looked so soft and deep, like you could sink into it, like maybe the knife had not punctured her flesh but only sunk into her fur. Of course there was all the blood, too.

There was a woman in a creamy dress with pearls seeded across her shoulders. It was her turn. She sat down in the grass next to the tiger and bent her knees. First she inserted her feet into the tiger. Then her calves, then her thighs. Then she lifted her butt so she could wiggle it inside. Someone near me made a small *oh* of either longing or grief. The lower part of the tiger carcass flipped around and you could tell the woman's feet were kind of cramped. Now she was entirely inside except for one arm, her shoulders, and her head. Based on her expression you couldn't tell what was happening to her. Something liquid and yellow-green was seeping through the pearls on her dress.

Now only her head was outside of the tiger. The knife man dropped the sheet of flesh he had been holding and made a joke motion as though he were zipping her up. Her face protruded right from the hollow of the tiger's throat, like a beautiful jewel or a second face.

From the side of the lawn people started pulling out the other animals they had already done. There was a walrus and a buffalo. There was a heartbreaking palomino horse. There was a reddish-gold bear big enough for two. People arranged them so they could be next to their friends. It became clear that everyone had buddies to sleep next to, while I had no one. I shrank back toward the aromatic trees.

"Wait!" A young woman with eyes like my own caught my wrist. "Please don't go."

By the afternoon Suya has to pee so badly that she can no longer avoid the bathroom. On the floor, the baby turns itself purple and blotchy with shrieking. They are both dunked in the noise. Suya would like to smack the baby in order to shut it up, but she knows if she does it will become hers, irrevocably. She will bear its broken weight for the rest of her life.

She releases her urine in a resentful flood. The baby arches upward in its bouncy chair like a fish caught on a line. It opens its mouth and unleashes an unbroken column of sound. Pink-tinged flecks fly from its mouth and land on the white cabinets, the shower curtain.

The toilet flush does nothing to inhibit its cries. Suya walks back into the bedroom. Closing her eyes she finds she can still picture the door half ajar, the darkness beyond. A cool breeze blows through the doorway and she shudders. She lifts one of the crone's sequin dresses from the floor and puts it on. It fits perfectly. The jeweled fabric has the slither of elegance and the heaviness of consequence. Her shoulders straighten.

In the bathroom the baby spits out yellow things and red things and brown things. Sometimes it chokes, and in those clogged seconds the air becomes completely still. Suya returns. She looks unstoppable in that dress. The single thought in her mind has birthed another, and another. Swollen purple clusters of thoughts, jostling and bursting and multiplying. There is wrenching silence as the baby gags on its own sounds. Suya trembles but does not slip. She bends down and plucks up the string of colorful wooden teething beads from the bouncy chair. She is careful not to touch the baby. She winds the beads around her neck like pearls.

Now she goes to the living room. She plucks the bloodied shawl from the crone's lap and drapes it over her own shoulders like a magnificent stole. The crone's hands tremble. Who knows what could be reacting within that inert flesh? Perhaps something remarkable. We'll never find out now.

The door slams. Suya! Follow her. Down five flights of stairs, out of the tower, onto the parched sidewalk. The street is silent except for her footsteps. Where is she walking? She's walking toward freedom. Or, rather, she's walking toward money. Oh, yes, that's it. She knows exactly where to go.

The young woman pulled me across the lawn. "We can share!"

We spooned each other inside her elk. Every part of my body was swaddled with either elk flesh or the woman's body. Slick clumps slid between my fingers. Stringy bits dried on my neck.

"I made something for you." The young woman extracted one arm from the carcass and dangled a charm bracelet in front of my face. I couldn't grasp it and so it fell into my mouth. It tasted cool and coated with putrefaction.

I spat it out. "I can't take that."

"But I've never met anyone like you before."

She tried to pull my wrist up to fasten the bracelet around it and I elbowed her away. In struggling I rotated so I faced the young woman. She wiped blood from her eyes and mouth and then my eyes and mouth. Her face brimmed with true kindness. "I think we could be friends."

The way she said it I knew it was true. We would never be bound by necessity, only inclination. I had never been given such a gift before. I could go home with her if I wanted. I could tell her what I had done and we could eat wild mushrooms fried in butter and absolve each other with friendship.

Either the notion or the stench of raw flesh was heady and I thought I would rupture.

"That's not what I want!"

I tried to push myself out of the sleeping bag, but I was so slippery I could not get purchase on anything. As I flailed it occurred to me that whether I accepted her or refused her, I could not hold myself apart. Why had I feared discovery? There was nothing to discover. Simply by reaching for power, I attained it. Simply by walking in, I became one of them.

She began to reminisce about our long acquaintance, how as children we rode a polo pony into the pool and it drowned. She was so rich the stories came true as she spoke them. My tears mingled with the viscera that pillowed my head. But I had thought I was choosing; just once, I had wanted to be a person who could choose.

The young woman hummed a familiar lullaby in my ear. The elk flesh held me as tightly as it had held the insides of the elk. Eventually I stopped shuddering. All around me people murmured to each other and wriggled reverently in their sleeping bags. Light fell down from the sky and brushed our faces with silver. Tomorrow we would rise from these skins and do everything we wanted. The sleepover had begun.

If You Lived Here, You'd Be Evicted by Now

THEY ALL CAME HOME TO kill Mama Erasmo and feed her heart to the foundations of the house. Casey and Stacy and Lorcom and Colin and Slug. Hadn't all been home together in years. It felt weird. Slug, seized by the fear of not recognizing anyone, considered bringing a sign to the airport, then rejected the idea in shame.

Like most reunions, this one was necessitated by zoning laws. Until they secured the house they might lose it at any moment to the predations of commercial adjustors. On the "Business or Personal" section of his flight reservation Casey delicately selected "Both."

Let's say there's no money in this world. Let's say if you want to obtain something, like rice or photocopies, you have to give somebody a handjob. Only nobody wants to give a hand-job in the grocery store or the copy shop, so instead at each register, in a clear glass tank, they have one of those giant clams from the Pacific Northwest, which is a symbol for genitalia. In lieu of payment you dip your hand into the cold salt water and caress the clam: once, twice.

Just kidding; of course there's money. Casey and Stacy both work in finance.

What does one need to kill one's mother? They basically cleaned out the hardware store. Surrounded by aisles of sharpening tools and different strengths of rope, Stacy worried she would run into someone from high school. Not that she had any reason to be ashamed. A standing desk exclusively for her use and a supportive partner: both of these awaited her return. Plus everyone came home on this errand sooner or later. She buried her anxiety in a shallow hole and walked away from it.

Colin and Lorcom stood close but not touching, contemplating a dusty display of candy bars discontinued before they had completed puberty. "If the world weren't so goddamn twisted, this could be kind of a celebration," one of them said.

"What about these?" Casey held up a pair of pruners with ergonomic hand grips to his siblings for approval. They glanced over and nodded. "They're on sale."

It's not that they had become inured to cruelty. Not at all. They took the shopping bags straight down to the basement and Mama didn't ask to see. The hometown weather was colder than had been forecast when they were packing and by evening everybody had augmented their outfits with last-resort layers dug out of childhood closets. Articles neither fashionable enough to have been borne with them nor cherished enough to be packed away in memory chests. Casey wore an I FINISHED THE AIRFORCE 5K sweatshirt, though he memorably hadn't. Stacy's wrists poked out of a sweater entirely too fuzzy, an entirely too girlish shade of purple. Just looking at her called into question her ability to reconcile herself with the world. Colin and Lorcom wore matching free giveaway tees from a local credit union. Slug, who had never moved out of the basement, sat cross-legged on the window seat, watching the rest of them from deep within the folds of a mothy fur coat.

Mama had failed to re-create their favorite dinner foods, but she had tried. There was cauliflower, steamed not roasted. There was chicken, though the skin puckered limply. The garlic had gone blue. They had expected eating to be more fraught, or imbued with poignant ritual, but it tasted just how it looked. They chewed with their mouths and swallowed with their throats. "I just feel like we aren't making the most of things!" You'd think that was Stacy but it was Casey. Everybody heard, nobody rose to do anything different. Really, transcendence never arrives at the moments you burden with meaning.

"Look, I'm not going to act like I'm glad this is happening," Mama said. "I'm not. I enjoy being alive. I go to sip-and-paint on Thursdays. My friend Jody's running for school board. I think she has a real shot. My avocado pit just grew a little shoot at the top, see it there? But also I'm not going to act like

I don't know how the world works. I knew how it would be when I got into all this." With a forkful of mashed florets she indicated that "all this" meant rearing five children. "It's not like I think you're enjoying it any more than me."

Except for Lorcom they all agreed they weren't enjoying it. Lorcom hoped his lack of enjoyment could be taken for granted. It felt somehow cheapening to assert your own detestation for murdering your mother.

A june bug battered the kitchen window screen. In the silence between blows, they each reached their own conclusions.

Somewhere, within one of their brains, a little thought shook itself off. I wonder how I will behave when the moment comes, it asked. I wonder if I will acquit myself nobly.

When they were children she referred to them all as "trooper." Come on, trooper, can't start the car until you're buckled. Chips or Oreos, trooper, not both. No, peroxide doesn't sting, trooper, no it doesn't.

Their childhood memories revealed a recurring theme of being admonished for impeding forward motion.

The house had been poorly constructed even before it became old. The basement flooded every spring when the snow melted. The big concrete porch on the front had been covered with toys and was still covered with toys, faded plastic configurations whose desirability they could no longer bring themselves to see. Rough patches on the floorboards where the cat had vomited before it died. Still they loved it the way you have to love the vessel of your childhood, without balance, all your pleasure yoked to an anchor point far behind you.

There were their bedrooms, one for girls where the ones who were girls slept, one for boys where the ones who were boys slept. Hard to remember who went where these days. On this night they ended up all in the same room, sleeping bags strewn about the floor. In their too-small clothes they looked like children feigning sleep. They looked incapable of grasping the task that lay before them.

Colin woke them up by hammering. Colin was definitively a boy. You could tell by how many things he broke and how many things he fixed. None of his siblings had ever put much time into getting to know him, yet they all assumed that when it came to the killing he would take the lead.

Mama had a list of tasks she hadn't gotten around to. It comforted her to watch Colin complete them, even at this late hour. The thermostat was stuck in Celsius. The spice racks had been stained but never hung. The dead bolt on the back door was bent from where an adjustor tried to kick it in last month.

"That's the kind of thing that won't happen once you kill me," Mama reassured Colin. "They'll know they can't touch it."

Colin was impressed by the rigor in her voice but did not know how to tell her. When he set down the hammer and turned to look at her, he found her staring out the window with her mouth cruelly tight. He thought maybe she had seen a car drive by that he had missed, that had angered her.

. . . .

It was a point of pride in the neighborhood that so far only three houses had become trading posts. That happened if you didn't kill your mother soon enough, or at all. One of the trading posts gave face massages and sold luxury lotions and herbal bath infusions. One of the trading posts was all local. One was a Waffle House.

There came a trickle of weekend shoppers seeking suitable gifts for vague acquaintances. They bought whipped-mud masks and wildflower honey and hash browns diced, chunked, and smothered. Some people you would only see inside the trading posts, never walking through the neighborhood. The servers at the Waffle House wore black balaclavas and took orders without speaking.

Look, I know it was the Thorntons' place, but my skin gets incredibly flaky this time of year, the neighbors justified to themselves. Can't really argue with convenience. Plus, they made their choice didn't they? It's not everything we need, sure, but you make do with what you have. No sense impeding forward motion. Get on with things.

It's not like they didn't feel grief. As they spoke about Mama, sometimes they caught themselves referring to her in the past tense already. An accident, it was an accident. "Practicing!" Lorcom joked drily, without needing anyone to laugh.

She was old but not that old. Sixty-six they thought and then tried not to. Her life was a drab gray thread when viewed from any significant distance, but up close it was variegated and lively and meant a great deal to her.

Sometimes she smoked weed on the weekends. Even when they were little. They could picture her standing on the porch with a joint in her left hand, clutching her terry robe closed with her right, yelling at them to watch out for dog shit in the leaf pile.

Casey, Stacy, and Colin had made it to college. Three out of five, nothing to be ashamed of. Lorcom was taken care of in a different way; one didn't ask. Slug checked a lot of political philosophy out from the library.

Colin left dinner early to do some final sharpening. Casey and Stacy cleared the dishes. Slug stayed sitting, leaned across the table to Mama.

"Don't you hate us?" said Slug. "Where is that inside you?"

Mama uncrossed her arms. "Look, honey, can you hate the sun for going down?" (Her tone like maybe if Slug weren't so, you know, maybe this explanation wouldn't be necessary.) She went on in her usual vein, what a miracle motherhood was, to willingly bring a creature into the world, to weep at its perfection, knowing one day it would end you.

In the kitchen, Casey, with suds on his wrists, brought up how Slug wasn't even biologically related to them anyway. They all remembered the circumstances under which Slug had come into their lives. Stacy shushed him. No need for that now. Besides, it wasn't biology that mattered, you know that. It was the manifestation of nurturance, which could look numerous ways.

Slug said nothing else for forty years.

It's not as though they were secretly brutes. It's not as though they took pleasure in carrying out hard but necessary tasks. It's not that their experience of pain was fundamentally different from ours. It's not that they were somehow more at peace with their instincts. It's not that it felt unreal, nor purely metaphorical. It's not that they did not know how to ask questions. It's not like this changed things irrevocably. It's not like nothing felt different. It's not that they were more monstrous than you. Nor were they more brave.

Stacy finished in the kitchen and creaked down the stairs to join her family. The sounds of the dishwasher gushed through the floor. They had inadvertently arranged themselves in a circle. Mama was no farther away from any of them than they were from each other, still she felt untouchably distant.

Let's say there's no shame in this world. Nothing holding you back, nothing at all. And still things did not come out how they wanted. No matter how well adjusted they imagined themselves to be—Casey liked to assure clients he could "tackle whatever those sons of bitches threw" at him—still they discovered seams in themselves that could be worked loose. They came undone.

They had lost ritual from their bones many generations ago, and they were all too averse to looking foolish to try and re-create it. There was a lot of patting each other on the shoulders, saying well, well now, here we are. If you think you will say exactly what you mean, in the moment when you must, you will be disappointed.

It's just how it was. Imagine you had to kill your mother. It was like that.

How to begin? They did not know, and then they already had.

. . . .

In the end she did fight back. Everybody does. She stopped being their mother at all; instead she was a red-hot wire of life, embedded within the flesh of a violent animal. You can't really comprehend this change until it happens. They loved her more then, not as their family but as a magnificent creature whose end they got to witness. They grew angrier and more determined to be worthy. It was more difficult than they had expected, because of the strength with which human tissues bind to each other, the myriad ways they can twist and dodge. They used every tool they had amassed. They even used the chain.

Let's say there's no heartbreak in this world. Let's say instead people just do a firm handshake and get on with things. Or if getting on feels impossible, you have the option of slicing off one of your formerly beloved's nipples and taking it with you as a souvenir. They are glad to let you do it. What a trinket to give up that the rest of their life might remain intact. Stacy wore four dried-out nipples threaded on a string around her neck. Over the course of the evening the four nipples were spattered with flecks of red becoming brown. Though when you looked more closely you saw they were only beads shaped out of pink clay, like a child might make. A friend's daughter. Perhaps this wasn't real either.

. . . .

When it was over they could not look at each other.

They dropped back into their bodies each alone. Their rationalizations had been inadequate, they realized. There was absolutely nothing that stood between them and the horror they had committed. They had held her heart in their hands, passed it around.

They sat on the floor and pinched at bits of dust. They reminded themselves of places they had heard of where things were very different, where you did not have to kill any of your own relations but instead lived with the knowledge in the back of your mind that a stranger, or several, in an unknown place had killed another stranger, or several, in order for you to live as you did. This seemed altogether more dishonest, and imprecise. They shivered at the thought and congratulated themselves for being so decent and so square.

Then they washed the thick blood and yellow streaks of bile from their hands. They bundled their clothes and set them in the incinerator, which had been replaced the previous fall with a quiet and efficient model.

They got up early the next morning and went for walks, alone or in pairs. The air was clear and frigid and felt the way it feels on vacation, untethered from the expectations of ordinary life.

They were struck by the realization that most of the other households in the neighborhood had completed the same task long before them. Lorcom watched a family jogging by—grandfather, two adult daughters, twin girls in a stroller—with astonishment. All this time you knew, and I did not. I moved through the world in ignorance. Now I know how it feels, and your composure that seemed so ordinary now seems miraculous. How can you—how can you not—

The family noticed Lorcom staring. But maybe they understood where his mind was (you had to, the screaming had carried all down the block), because they nodded politely and turned a corner.

In this way they came to understand that it was not impossible to go on. They would learn to bear it. Their skin was thicker and more elastic than they had suspected; it could conceal beneath itself unimaginable transformations. They felt cleansed by this awareness, propelled forward by unexpected energy. They returned to the house preceded by their long shadows cast by the rising sun. Each motion they made felt new, and newly precise.

They were in the kitchen, there was just enough chicken left for five sandwiches, a knock came on the door.

"Here to complete the adjustment," said the little man to Colin, whose knuckles whitened around the doorknob. Stacy froze the mayonnaise knife above a slice of bread.

Finally Lorcom managed, "We've secured the place. You can't."

The adjustor was having difficulty with his clipboard and tablet and stylus and phone all in two hands. His nose a little fruit in front of his softened face. At their words the fruit ripened. "Not possible."

Colin, grayly, recollected his language. "Of course not"—his shrug had a tinge of retch—"but there it is."

"I won't meet my quota."

The adjustor had not meant to say this, they could tell. It was the involuntary reaction to a moment of unexpected distress. How trivial his distress, how mean and opportunistic compared to their own sonorous loss. They grew desperate to get rid of him; he polluted their meditations on grief.

Get out, their hisses implied. They could basically move as one organism now. *Get out.* Now the blue embers of their hearts were cased in glass. As was the house. "*Get out!*" Picture five resplendent snakes hissing from one hole.

"Of course—I'm sorry! I'm sorry." And his hands held up, palms out, demonstrated that he was.

Their faceted eyes watched him as he retreated from the door.

He kept his hands up until he was back out on the sidewalk, out of the shadow of the house. He scanned the street, afraid that someone had seen. The sound of the deadbolt sliding shut made him jump. He glanced back at the front window and saw a corner of a curtain twitch, then fall into place. He brought his arms down slowly to his sides, conscious of every joint articulated in the process. The street was empty. The brightness of the day repercolated into his awareness. Birds resumed singing.

His name was Merclaire and he did not relish the hunt. A counselor in the GED program had recommended the adjustor profession as a "ladder straight to the top," though in retrospect Merclaire realized, as he often did, that he had misunderstood.

He stood for another moment outside the Erasmo house until the sting of their eyes subsided, then he relocated to the end of the block. His heart was not racing but he breathed heavily. A high cold sun left the air bright and heatless. The breeze chilled his bald spot.

His key jammed in the bike lock and he nearly sobbed. He would not meet his quota. The event so long flickering on his horizon had finally come to pass. *This really is your final chance, Merclaire.* He was hopeless at repossessing houses but adroit at convincing himself he could make it work out. Now the true ramifications tumbled into his awareness. Somehow the adjustment gods would be placated. If all the roster houses had been secured, his own home became eligible for sacrifice. Imagining his house as a trading post made a ruthless physical impulse rise up in him. Though he understood he was embedded in a scheme designed for him to fail, still he could not eradicate the feeling of personal incompetence. Shame sat in his gut like a Lego block.

His wife had recently been promoted from driver to clerk at the transportation bureau. She took night classes on administration. His daughter Havana had been born on the kitchen floor, Havarti in the bathtub. Such a relief to watch them roll around. Finally, people who would never fully grasp how far he had traveled to meet them.

Unable to bear acceleration, he walked his bike toward home.

Look up at the sky. Had there ever been such a saturated blue, so harmed by contrails? Merclaire could only concentrate on his own fear. His own mother had died a decade ago and her heart, though generous while alive, had not been of use to anyone. Maybe he could kill another relative who provided equivalent nourishment. Maybe he could locate the part of his body that cared for himself and cut it off. Watch that a setback in one area does not trigger catastrophic thinking everywhere, his therapist had said, but the court didn't pay for therapy anymore.

Without noticing the journey, he had pushed the bike to the top of the hill dividing the Erasmos' neighborhood from his own. His body was coldly layered in sweat. Here there was no sidewalk, only the crumbling edge of the asphalt, demarcated from the driving lane by a white line. He could feel the crushing weight of the cars in the breeze they made as they passed.

Behind him, neat though worn houses. Frost-damaged azaleas. Cars on concrete pads. Ahead of him, a tire yard, a parking lot for a moving company. Blocks of gray apartment buildings. His house shared a wall with a nail salon. So far the daughters seemed unbothered by the fumes.

To the left he could see all the way down to the business district of the city. He paused here, from dread or admiration. He liked to stand with the girls on this hill and invent conversations for the city people. What's your favorite animal? How about your favorite color? Did you draw that? What did you have for snack today? At this distance the buildings appeared innocuous, finely wrought miniatures. The malevolence that hung over them like smog dissipated before it could reach his nostrils. They emitted a great threat in their twinkling but from here he could imagine his family unscathed.

Trash flipped in the alley to his right. A noise like a raccoon stuck in a can. The incongruity of vision and reality was unsustainable. He swung a leg over the bike and descended in a rush, cold peeling his knuckles.

. . . .

His wife sat on the porch of their duplex with two men. Merclaire had not realized her brothers would get out of prison so soon. They looked smaller than he expected men returning from prison to look, dapper in white T-shirts and elastic-waisted pants. They had spent their time bettering themselves.

The men faced the house; his wife surveyed the street from her chair and so saw him first. He noted in her shoulders the moment she realized he bore bad news. Perhaps he lost focus or maybe he willed it; the bike's front tire slipped from the sidewalk into the grass and could not regain its tread. The handlebars hit concrete with a clatter that made the brothers turn around. Under his pants his scraped leg smarted.

A rattle of paper—a Burger King bag stuck to his shoe. He shook it off and told them what had happened.

"I can't make quota now. I needed that one."

His wife's face did not collapse. Her voice carried only the exhaustion it usually did. "They'll—" and that was all she said. *Come for the house,* was the rest of her statement. He heard anyway, the words coalescing in the air in puffs of icy mist.

They'll come for the house.

There was nothing between security and precarity. You lived in one and then you lived in the other. The wet soft body of a newly molted cicada takes only a moment to dry in the sun. He watched her harden toward their new future at the same time he felt it in himself. What will I do, what will I do, he had wondered, pedaling home. Now he thought, there is no depth to which I would not plunge the knife.

"Terrible, the multiple emotional valences occupied by the idea of home," said one of the brothers. They had just passed through the portal from prison back into the world; some strange ideas were bound to slip in with them. They all turned their heads at the same moment to look at the walls of the duplex. He loved it the way you must love a home, without volition, as a proxy for all the larger secret structures in which you were housed. It kept them dry, it withstood tornadoes. In the salon next door a disco ball whirled.

His wife glanced down at her own breasts, contemplating herself as an object. No, it was out of the question. The daughters could not yet cut their own hotdogs, much less overpower an adult woman.

His wife's name was Lousi. Merclaire felt frequently on the verge of becoming irrelevant to her. Nightly her mind went off on trajectories whose endpoints remained undisclosed. She liked him to tuck in the girls while she cleaned the kitchen. Then she'd stand with her hands submerged in soapy water. After two stories and a lullaby he would join her, reach from behind her to slip a spoon into the sink and pull his hand back with a hiss. The water on his fingertips was so hot it felt like his skin had melted and slid off. Like the suds sloshed against raw nerve. Lousi turned her head a little toward him, hands still submerged, face tranquil—"Sorry, did you say something?"

The brothers conferred. The taller brother detached himself from the porch railing. Flecks of white paint stuck to his forearm.

"We have a proposal. If you are willing."

He looked delicately concerned. Lousi's eyes narrowed.

The brother continued, "We have a personal connection. An enterprising young lady. She works as a surrogate."

Lousi had a particular noise of exasperation reserved for her relations. "Not another—"

"I have the utmost faith in her practices."

"You expect us to just—"

"It's Tohn's cousin, Lousi. It could be beneficial for everyone involved."

"Beneficial, he says!"

The brother steepled his long fingers. "I don't bring it up lightly."

Merclaire fixated on the brother's fingernails. Pink ovals with thin even white rims. Years ago when he had first visited Lousi's family, that same brother had socked him in the face with a bag of deer's blood fertilizer. Merclaire found himself unable to imagine the experience of prison.

He took two steps up to the porch. "I can do it."

Lousi looked dubious. "Baby, you don't—"

The brother not speaking was texting intently. "She can be here this evening, if you like."

Lousi twisted and twisted and twisted the muscular braid of her hair. All the ties which Merclaire had been led to believe would bind her to him turned out to have little hold. She was looking at them all and then for an instant she was looking at none of them.

"I can't skip class tonight." Regret and relief chased each other through her voice.

He shook his head. "I'll take care of it."

He shook his head. "It'll be fine."

The taller brother spread his hands out as though he were balancing two columns of sky. The appreciation of basic freedom still radiated from him. "If you have any doubts, we're happy to—"

Merclaire remembered the Erasmo children staring at him from within the dim cave. Their faces orphaned and dangerous. Do you know, each of them had taken a turn with the heart. They had grated it against the exposed cinder block of the basement until the pericardium was shredded to fluff. They had pried a stone up out of the floor and set what remained underneath.

He shook his head. "No. Of course not. I understand."

In the evening they fed the daughters creamed corn and waited. Havana and Havarti were two and four and still assessing the boundary between self and decorum. They poked their creamy forklets into each other's mouths and cheeks and hair. He swooped them into the tub, enthralled them by scooping water in a cup and pouring it from a high distance.

Then Lousi had departed for class and the girls had departed into sleep. Merclaire rocked on the porch. He dreaded this hour after their bedtime, the way the quiet advanced. He never felt confident he could retrieve himself from it.

There is so much to the world that is not seen or felt, he thought. The light and limp breeze and distant traffic noise remained the same, yet everything was different. Their home, the daughters, the high chair, the kitchen with its yellow walls, the beadboard and the linoleum siding, in a day it had all become improbably flimsy. A clot of sticks floating down a river, just barely cohered through the motions of chance and water. On all sides tumbled tires and segments of infrastructure and more massive flotillas of junk. At any moment something could collide with their nest and scatter everything as thoroughly as if it had never existed.

He rode the speeding island with the bravura of insolvency. It sailed around a bend and he found himself whirling toward a girl, submerged to her waist in the middle of the river, her arm sheathed to the pit in the throat of a monstrous fish.

He jerked awake; gnats departed his arm hairs. Rocked his wife's porch chair until he could reincorporate himself. The sky at the top of the street was deepening, white to orange to blue.

Two bikes crested the hill in staggered formation. The trailing one ridden by a bulky two-headed creature. Merclaire squinted and this resolved itself into the shorter brother, with a stranger perched behind him on the pegs. As they descended the stranger let go of the brother's shoulders and stretched her arms out to the sides. The dark shadow of their combined forms spread its wings, swooped down the long hill.

The brothers parked their bikes and unloaded gear from the panniers. Something bulky, jointed metal pieces wrapped in canvas. A slender scuffed tool case. They bore both up the stairs into the house, following the pointing of the stranger's hand. Merclaire nodded as they passed but the brothers' eyes had narrowed to business and they were unable to respond.

Up close his understanding revised again: she was so bulky and misshapen because of the coat she wore. A pillowing of winter parka with a giant hood mounded on her shoulders. Meanwhile he had on only a windbreaker. At her approach he broke into sweat all over, a cold rubbery layer that chafed his armpit as he raised a hand in uncertain greeting.

"What can I say, I'm a heat creature." She spoke to his silent thoughts from within the burrow of her hood. A round dark face he barely saw, thick wings of eyeliner. Beads of sweat crawled down his neck. She tickled his outstretched fingers as she passed—a handshake? Dap? Low five? Then the door of his house was closing, and she was inside and he was out.

"This is Tohn's cousin." The brother making introductions looked impatient to be proven right.

This time the cords of her wrist stood out as she wrung his hand. "Jessyup."

Despite the lines around her eyes Jessyup could not have been more than twenty-one. Her coat hatched to reveal a soft mustardy dress and black leggings. Merclaire was unskilled in interpreting the outfits of young people—did this clothing suggest going out, or staying in, or participating in some kind of athletic event?

She embarked on an impressive choreography of explanation and arrangement; indifferent words belied by crisp motions. He marveled at how such opposed mechanisms of self-preservation could coexist.

"We do the, we call it the parturition, first." Simultaneously she telescoped the table's metal legs and snapped them into place. "For the mother part. Then, make sure it sticks? Then the, like, matricide." Sitting on the joint of the folding table, she jogged her weight until they heard a click. "The killing part." The stirrups at the end of the table remained folded.

She clipped a cheap work lamp to the arm of his chandelier, wrapped her hands around the table end, and scudded its rubber feet two millimeters to the left. One millimeter to the right. He had never before seen a spell cast; still he recognized its presence.

The pad of her thumb clicked on the lamp. The light was soft and warm but aggrieved his mind like a nail. He could not recall what hung on his own walls. Drawings from the girls? Of what? All of the house outside the glow was called into question. The brothers, standing on either side of the kitchen door, were shadowy pillars. Now she laid a sheet over the table and her tone was so offhand he knew it would be okay.

He managed, "Is there anything to sign?"

He could have sworn her tone of voice turned wistful. "No."

As though on a long fog-obscured road, he looked back over his shoulder. He saw behind him the line that held back his old life from this hidden zone, demarcated in blood. He had not noticed when he crossed the border, but looking back, yes, perhaps he had felt it.

Jessyup extracted the tools from her case. A plastic squeeze bottle. A knife, the blade curved and nearly blue. A flat metal plate with a half-moon cut in the middle.

"For the parturition, only part of you needs to come out of me. More substantial the better, but, uh—we strike a balance. Most people use a foot." She gestured helpfully to Merclaire's feet. "Then for the matricide, you take this"—the curved knife—"right here"—the meatless plane of her sternum. "And I got the guard"—the perforated metal plate—"so don't worry about taking too much off."

She scooted herself onto the table. Without him noticing she had peeled off her black leggings. Now she sized up her yellow dress, clicked her tongue. "Didn't come here prepared. Thought I was going to Ellen's."

He said, "No, you don't have to," as she shucked the dress over her head.

"Don't want blood on it." Then folded it with an attention to seams that he associated with middle age.

The light altered the landscapes of her bare skin but her manner was unchanged. Scars, some pale, some pink and fresh, dappled her chest like leaf shadows. She crouched to inspect something inside the case. Her genitals obscured by her folded shins. Merclaire was acutely aware of his own dense body. Even his shoulders sprouted hair.

She looked up and frowned, as though gauging the correct aperture through which to view him. "You need to take your shoes off."

Her eyes were hard, granular. He wondered what part of yourself you had to banish in order to get that look, and where you sent it to.

"Hey! Focus." When she opened her mouth he saw not a tongue but a stretch of flat gray water, reflecting the black branches of trees overhead. She nodded. "Some people need a minute." She buffed the knife with a gray microfiber cloth. "Know why my cousin's in jail?"

He didn't know.

"You don't know. Fishing!"

Fishing!

"They didn't like him fishing how he did. Believe that bullshit?"

He couldn't believe. He worried he wasn't hearing her correctly and scooted his stool closer. Sitting again on the table her legs dangled, her toes brushed the surface of the river.

"He'd take me with him sometimes. They make their holes in the silt. Catfish. You do it all with your hands."

She stretched a hand out to him. He almost but not quite moved to take it. Each goose bump on her arm possessed a distinct shadow.

"What he taught me was, it's all about confidence. You find a hole and then you reach until you feel the mouth. Doesn't take much. The fish can't help himself, he wants to clamp down. He wants to feel something inside him."

Where she was from the catfish lived for centuries. They grew as large as children. The people who lived by the water understood fish the way they understood their own limitations. They knew how to walk to the river door and knock.

By the time Jessyup was eight her gift was plain. Her cousin Tohn would end up in prison but she was the true transgressor. She would squat in the opaque muck of the river, face tilted to the sky, eyes glassy and unnecessary. While below the surface her hands performed an intricate petition. The fish snuggled in the mud. She brushed its forehead. The fish declined and curved back toward its unknowable life. Her fingers skipped in pursuit and grazed a query along its lip. Her touch as light as the breeze that bows the wheatfield hairs along your arm. The fish, appalled, entranced, assented, unbolted the garage of itself. With the pads of her fingers she discovered where the bony rim of its mouth gave way to slick rippling ridges.

Tohn sat on the dock end, knocking the pylons with his heels, flecking the water with picked scabs. He watched his baby cousin in the water, her face at first blank with concentration, then spreading into a smile. A slow unfurling of satisfaction. She was not in yet but she would be, she knew. She would not be refused.

And then—*there.* She punched her hand all the way down its throat. Strata of muscles convulsed around her arm like a new atmosphere. The creature recoiled but could not regain itself. They moved as one organism bound by red-hot wires, the flesh of a single violent animal. She tilted her body into its pitch and heave as her hand worked its way deeper, seeking the place where soft flesh gave way to air.

And then—*there.* Her fingers reemerged through the slit of its gills. She clasped her two hands together so the massive creature was threaded onto her embrace.

In a rush she straightened her legs, rose from the river. Water streamed from her sopping hair, brown shoulders, blue bikini. She bore the fish up with her, still threaded on her arms, still hurling itself toward escape. In a smooth motion she heaved it over her shoulder so its pale belly shone to the sky. With its flank pressed to her face she could see its white scales glittering every color. They took the light and gave it back in pieces. Its massive body smelled of murk and innards. Its slime flecked in her eyes. She braced her feet, waited for it to thrash. Her breath deepened, exulted. It's not that she's a brute, though. It's not that the fish is a beast. It's not that she finds purest joy in the conquest of another body—no wait, it is. It is.

"Hey, Tohn," she called, laughing. "Tohn, watch!"

She drew one hand back into the sheath of its body. Negotiated anatomy. Then, radiant in the sunlight, the silhouette of her hand took shape, pressing outward from inside the belly of the fish. Five fingers and a palm, rising from the taut white flesh like a creature straining to escape.

"Here." Jessyup smacked into his hand a bottle of icy blue jelly. "Use this. Be liberal."

He was still there, under the bare bulb in the dark room. The vapors of her story lingered in the shadows, dissipated. The bottle had no brand name but several labels' worth of fine-print warnings. He assumed it had come from a multipack. He felt close to the true shape of his pain. As crisp and revolting as the outline of a girl's hand pressing through the white belly of a fish. He inverted the bottle and ejected a mound of blue gel into his palm.

He had forgotten to peel off his sock; now he had to do it one-handed. He tried to raise his foot while standing, teetered, steadied himself on the table where she sat. Black shreds of lint stuck in the humid crevices of his toes. The pile of lubricant slid around in his palm. He denied himself a glance back to see if the brothers watched.

He slicked down the hairs of his ankle with blue gel. It did not sting but he nonetheless perceived pain.

As Jessyup went to recline on the table her hand slipped off the edge. She fell toward him and instinctively his hand caught her shoulder. His thumb pressed into the dip of her collarbone. The hand-shaped area of contact between them grew warm. Jessyup observed his grip on her shoulder and nodded with thin lips. "Okay."

I didn't say anything at the time, but did you hear how hard Slug cried? Huge shuddering sobs that could engulf a whole person, that could swallow a body like a well and give back only water. Through the whole thing. See, there is grief immense enough to convert you into something other than a solid, something incapable of wielding any tool. See, there is nothing new in this story after all. They want only what we want. The heart that is also the house. The arm of another wound through our own lungs so that goose bumps rise along its wrist every time we take a breath.

It's worth noting that even now, Merclaire never stopped believing in the possibility of kindness. Perhaps not for him or for her, but for someone, somewhere, the gentlest route was being taken.

Let's say in this world there is a ledger somewhere, in which this persistent faith is noted down. Let's say it matters.

She arranged her heels in the stirrups. Her vulva was tinted with the same blue jelly as his foot. He felt the clench of something around his heart. And his heart was the handle to all the rest of him, and so held him paralyzed.

He said, "I can't do this."

She said, "You must, or else they will shoulder you from your home and throw your babies to the asphalt and rain your belongings down from the windows onto your heads."

She said, "You must, because you cannot avoid it. You must see by now. Violence is like matter, neither created nor destroyed, it only changes form."

She said, "You must, you promised Lousi."

Just kidding. She shrugged and fished a pulp of pizza crust from behind a back tooth. Said, "Oh, come the fuck on." She propped herself on her elbows and let her head fall back. Her face looked toward the ceiling and her eyes looked beyond. Her knees were pitched open. Her chest heaved. "Quit acting like you're saving somebody."

Merclaire did not see her expression so he did not know which way she meant it.

He lifted his foot. His ankle bore the weight of all the silence in the room.

He set his foot down again. "I can't."

Jessyup spoke from a distant riverbank. "Of course you can."

He lifted his foot.

He set his foot down again.

He lifted his foot.

Ultimate Housekeeping Megathrill 4

Just look at her, dozing at the conveyor belt with her chin almost thunking her chest. Mouth slightly open, spit strand spanning her cracked lips. Her arms dragging like seaweed in a warm tide. All the while a river of junk flows past her, unexamined. Wake up Offie you are missing some *real treasures!* Offie is Initial Quality Control, see. Without her the Initial Quality would just go spiking all over the map, and what would everybody do then? It's not like the waste items will just separate themselves out of the reclamation stream. (Those days, kiddo, are past.)

Offie yawns. *Yaaaawwwwwwnnnnnn.* The strand of saliva breaks as her lips part. She winches her eyes open. Her vision all blurry and flecked with yellow crud. She wipes the crud away (with the wrists, remember, not the hands! The hands are coated in pale blue sanitary gloves and we all know what those gloves encounter) and then she stands for another moment, shoulders just barely rise-and-falling.

She doesn't look left or right. If she did, she would see similarly zoned-out persons on either side of her, wearing similarly stained canary-yellow jumpsuits. Three more such people sway on the other side of the conveyor belt. (Initial Quality Control, obvi, is not a job entrusted to just one single saggy dozer lady.) She doesn't look ahead or behind. If she did she would see the conveyor belt meander away through the vastness of the warehouse, branch into four daughter belts, chunter the mixed paper up a series of rollers, spew the remainder off a cliff so it clatters down in a waterfall of plastic/glass/metal. She doesn't see the belts that slink low under magnetic panels so that the tin cans leap out like mad salmon from a river. She doesn't see the distant, even more zoned canaries, whose sole purpose in life is to scrape away the metal junk clinging to the walls.

Most of all, Offie doesn't look up. Up is where the claws hang, and Offie decided on her first day at this luckytoget job that she never needed to set her eyes that way. Within a week she understood it didn't matter, she could have come to work blindfolded. The claws call forth new eyes from the back of your head. They brush their precision-tipped pincers over the tender hairs on the back of your neck. *We are sleeping lightly*, they rasp, swaying as a rare breeze wends through the warehouse. *We are waiting for you to fail.*

No, Offie keeps her eyes glazed in front and a little down, as though she can see through the conveyor belt to something hidden beneath. After this many years she could do the job with empty sockets. All on their own her hands dart out to snag a metal muffin tin, a coil of AV cable.

Across the conveyor belt, another canary squints at Offie. "Something keeps you up last night?" This canary is called Silene (though the facility is too cheap-o to embroider such letters on her jumpsuit) and her arms fly around the belt like she's moshing old-school hardcore. Bit of an Initial Quality Control-Freak, is Silene. She is hands down number-one hall-of-fame garbage-snatcher, except for once every two weeks, the day before her next paycheck comes in, when she runs out of the labor enhancers she injects into her armpits. Then she sways on her feet like a goon.

Offie drags her eyes up to Silene's face. Offie hasn't run out of labor shooters. Offie is just tired, genuine all-natural tired. She raises her eyebrows and sucks in her lower lip and hopes that her face gives Silene all the answer she needs. Silene does a shrug with her eyeballs. "Sure-kay, then. Whatever."

Their arms never stop moving.

"Maybe cause her daughter runs off and gets knocked up." This squawked from somewhere upstream. Who knows which canary; it's not important.

Offie swings her head sideways like the preparatory arc of a wrecking ball. "What?"

Every canary on the line goes silent. They are very busy fishing out nonrecyclables, oh yes, look there, is that some Styrofoam, oh no, just crumpled paper, well you never know, doesn't hurt to check, it's what we're here for after all. Et et et cetera.

Offie turns from the conveyor belt. She steps off the line. Trudges upstream toward the other canaries. "You are asking. About. My family?"

Hard to tell here if Offie is issuing a first warning or calling down a blight from the angels of despair. Her children would know, but they have not yet made their entrance. The workers decide as a matter of workplace safety that her question must have been rhetorical. From under a pile of computer parts they wrest out an enormous plush tiger spouting fiberfill from his jugular. Offie huffs again. Her exhalation dislodges the earwax from everybody's ears.

And their supervisor rounds the corner: "Everybody doing good here? Ofelie? Mikram? Hmm . . . ?"

What good timing this dude has. He claps Offie on the back. Nods to another canary and glances vaguely at the rest of them (hoping to skip over the fact that he has forgotten/never learned their names). They understand this trailing off as a small courtesy and avert their eyes.

Offie spins around to avoid his hand. "You are not touching me, Navid, mm-*no*."

"Ofelie. You're completely out of station."

"One of them steps on her family, Mr. N," Silene contributes. (What is this, kindness, from Silene? Has her midday shot of HotProle flooded her with temporary solidarity?)

Supervisor Navid looks torn. "I get that, but . . . At the end of the day . . ." He probes his hairline with two fingers. "You have to stay in your station, Ofelie. What am I supposed to do?"

Offie meets the man's eyes. She will never admit it, but this Navid is not bad, as supervisors go. She knows how it could be. Oh sure, he is mopped with self-importance. Sure, his pores ooze productivity-seminar jargon. Sure, his meat is soaked in slow disenchantment with his role that manifests in erratic bouts of cruelty. And yet, and yet. At the center of all that, Offie can see it: a desiccated clot of kindness. It pulses bloodlessly within him.

He shifts his fingers to massage back and forth between his eyebrows.

Offie does one full-body sigh to end all sighs. "Kay, Navid. All you gotta say."

She walks back to her place on the belt. Supervisor blinks like he can't believe his victory came so easily. "Oh, well. Well thanks, Ofelie. Ms. Ferdinand. Thank you. I don't mean to . . . It's just . . . the *pressure* we're under. Election coming up. Winds shifting . . . you know what I mean. They repeal the law, those guys come back down . . ." He gestures vaguely up at the claws. (No one ever points directly at the claws; they grow stronger when named.) "Won't be anything I can do for you then . . ."

No need to tell that to the canaries. Like they could ever forget. The claws were faster and stronger and to deprive them of water breaks or sufficient ventilation was no problem-o. Choke Silene full of enhancers like a foie-gras duck and she still would not control quality at one-tenth the rate of a freshly lubricated all-digital waste auto-sorting unit. *Go ahead,* rasp the claws. *Try to become us. Try as hard as you like. Rip away every piece of yourself; we will still be here.*

Offie makes a noise like please could we move on now. Upstream another canary overturns a yogurt tub and shrieks. Out has tumbled a bolus of rotting meat, leaking green juice, writhing with maggots. (That's what those blue gloves are for, ladies!) The conveyor belt chugs on, its motor-song so deep and pervading it stopped being sound long ago. It is feeling now. It is the vibration in the background of their bones. When Offie leaves work at night, she notices not silence but stillness.

Supervisor thumps his fist against a panel on the support column behind Offie. It re-lights. White letters on a blue background: Reclamation Center 3301—Celebrating 40 Years of Waste-Free Society!

Offie doesn't need to turn to know what it says. What, you think she hasn't stood before this panel every day for the last thirteen years? You think those letters aren't burned into the back of her brain? Her hands never stop burrowing, flipping, sorting. Blue light from the screen glistens on the layer of meat slime that coats her wrists, her knuckles, the webs of her thumbs.

The end of the day. The bus ride home. Breathe, finally. The bus skims twenty stories above the ground, red sunset light cuts in horizontally. Offie shades her face with one tepid hand. Maybe the clatter of the bus is supposed to massage but it only draws her aches deeper. Never took an anatomy class but this lady here can name each individual muscle by how it cries to her in the evenings. Cramps zipper up her calves, crowbar the base of her skull.

The bus heaves forward through sun-thickened air. Empty big-box stores and self-storage parks roll away underneath. There on the left, housing subdivisions creep into view. From above they make patterns like paisley screened on cheap cotton. Soured houses and cul-de-sacs rubbled by weeds.

Burb-burb-ba-durb. The official line for this place is that no one lives here anymore. Get it? The bus is full of slumped and cranky no ones. The vacant lots host no one, trading gossip with no one else. No one scuffs the eroding sidewalks, no one buys fakecakes from the cart on the corner. And in the handicapped seat of the bus, one flagrantly unhandicapped no one—her legs stretched out, her hand to her face—tries to peer out the window without looking like she's looking. Thinks: *My daughter is down there somewhere. Celado. Cece. Number-one baby girl. Perhaps at this very moment I am gliding over her head.*

The bus spirals down to the station and she turns inward, zones her eyes again on the blank in-between.

Psst. Here. Let's go somewhere different for a moment. Don't worry. It's only a game.

There is a cream-colored house with a steeply gabled roof and a porch that wraps around three sides. She stands on the sidewalk in front of it; it is her house. It is not spotless; the paint peels in places and the kitchen window has a spiderweb, but she does not mind. The shutters are new anyways, painted a deep Greek blue with little star-shaped holes cut into them. Multiple sets of wind chimes hang in the porch, including the lumpy clay ones made by one of her daughters in a fifth-grade pottery unit. There is a new rocking chair on the porch also, which the game refers to as "Mission-style." She will sit there later; it is a good seat from which to husk some corn.

She readjusts the grocery bag on her hip. A breeze shifts the leaves overhead. The street behind her is freshly paved and the fall bite in the air is cut by the chemical tang of tar. Her vegetables are damp from the mister; she should get inside before the bag tears. It is only that she likes to stop and look at it sometimes. The house. The garden with the witch hazel erupting in yellow lace. It brings to her a feeling broader than joy, more like fullness; a better use for the word *fullness* than anything she has felt from consuming a meal. She imagines the fish who build their nests on the seafloor, shifting sand back and forth with their bellies. Slowly they create a wallow deep enough to submerge themselves. She is like that, very gently nudging herself into the earth. It is a safe place she has made, safe for everyone. She is warm enough from her own fullness that the cool edge to the breeze does not bother her. With one hand she fishes her keys from her purse and starts up the front walk.

Nice thoughts aren't they, honey child? Ha, Offie's real home is no such thing. From the bus station she crosses the cracked remains of a highway and enters the burbs. The mouth of her street marked by a faux-rock sign embossed with huge curlicue letters: Colt's Brook Estates. Many subsequent strata of genitalia spray-painted over the words. Some of the houses here were completed and have begun the long slow slide into decrepitude, but most never got the chance to begin. Abandoned mid-construction, looming up like weathered whale skeletons from the barren earth.

People are out on their dirt lawns, sucking down the evening. They perch on stoops or sprawl in dismantled wheelie cars. Someone heys, "Miss Ofelie!" but Offie can't tell where the voice comes from. "Miss Ofelie, you need an expansion pack?" A lady about her age hustles on the curb. Holds out a clear bag with three blue marbles inside. "I get it from my sister-in-law. Perfect, mm, perfect. Makes you go, why do I ever play without this one?" Offie pauses, squints at it for two seconds, waves lady hustler away. "Mm-mm, I'm happy with what I got. Can't get greedy, you know?"

Lady shrugs and retreats. Deal won't last long. Offie plods on. On a plume of breeze comes the smell of grilling patties.

. . . .

Offie's actual house is so identical to every other house it doesn't matter what it looks like. No garden (ha-*ha*), no house numbers, no nothing. Only uniqueness is the pattern of seams that water leaks have opened up in the vinyl siding. The prefab panels buckle and slip into a network of brown lines like an angry face. To clarify: it is not Offie's house to own. Every month, payment flows to the account of a dried-apple-faced landlady who brews grey-market organs in the scuffed remains of a stainless-steel kitchen. How can it be like that, you wonder? What supply and demand jacks up the rents of the badland burbs? None, obvs. It is nothing but the way it's always been. From the taste-makers' quarter, demand for Offie's existence is you don't even know how low. All while the supply of Offies remains sky, sky high.

Offie steps into what was once a foyer. Once people knew the word *foyer.* Once the floor boards were some cheerful economical wood, oak or maple or whatever. Now they warp like driftwood. Once there was a chandelier dangling from the two-story ceiling. Now there is only an ugly black pimple and some singed eels of wire.

Offie turns right and starts up the stairs. The banister hangs by two screws. Along the hallway are two other rented rooms, an over-shared bathroom, and a doorless area their landlord refers to as "*la biblioteca*" without any evident acknowledgment of irony.

There's light behind the door at the end of the hall. What was once the door to the master bedroom. What is now the door to the entire abode of the entire Ferdinand family. She keys the makeshift deadbolt and heaves her shoulder against the sticky wood once, twice, before it sproings open.

The room is big for a room, but for a five-person home? Tiny, yo. In one corner the standard subsistence setup, round table with a crack down the middle, white plastic shelves stacked with commodity boxes, fry pan, hot plate, water tank. In the opposite corner two futons covered by faded safari-print sheets. (Don't need to sit on those futons to know the motherlode of crumbs hidden in their creases.) In the alcove that overlooks the front yard, a black vinyl armchair. Its arms are shiny with grime, the clutches of a bazillion hands over years polishing smooth their own scum.

On the futon closest to the door—what's this? Someone's genmod project, pre-assembly? The brutal welding of Angus steer + ape helices? No, no. Only (ostensibly) a young man. His head rests on a stuffed pink hippopotamus. With one hand he swipes games on a screen. He has traces of Offie in the tilt of his chin, the way his feet angle out. Siphon off all of Offie's exhaustion, replace it with spring-loaded ire, you might be able to guess this honcho here is her oldest child.

She named him Floro; when he was born, the whole world seemed about to bloom.

Nineteen years later she does not glance his way as she comes home.

Floro's only motion as his mother enters is to lazily extract his other hand from his pants. Announces the gesture by snapping his waistband against his stomach. Offie heads for the water jug.

Floro drops the screen, tracks her with suddenly sharp eyes. "I see Cece this morning."

Offie fills a cup and keeps her lips zipped. She plants her hands onto the table and just *leans* for a moment. All the pressure of the day percolates down through her body. She takes one deliberate breath. In-two-three. Out-two-three.

Floro swings his legs off the futon. "She's staying over in Fox Dales. Mom? She looks not so good. All big in the gut and thin in the eyes, you know?"

Offie takes another breath. She squinches her eyes closed, savors the feeling of her eyeballs trapped inside her head. "One-son. Do not. Bring up that trashdaughter before I even have a second to rest. How about?"

Floro does a big deal of rubbing his mouth and rolling his eyes. "*Mom*."

Offie does the thing she's best at; she shuts him out. High-density number-one son, all rhomboids and deltoids and trapezii and biceps. Might be a half-inch shorter than his mama but he's gonna use every bit of body he's got. Been thrashing his own muscles since before he had a deep voice. He is sinewed and corded and streamlined as a dolphin—yet still, perched atop the taut mass of his torso: a face like an unkissed debutant. Dreamy long eyelashes. Cut strawberry mouth.

Offie blurs him as easily as she blurs conveyor belts, bus tableaus, the black puckery mildew on the ceiling. Within her circle of focus she allows: the table, the cup.

Floro stalks across the room, pushes into her field of vision. Pale fairyking eyes welling with frustration. Believe it, boy has gotten people to do terrible things with those eyes. "You're icing out a fourteen-year-old girl?" Their noses almost touch. "Aren't you the adult, huh? Aren't you the all-grown-up *woman*."

WHACK, she slaps him. Like slapping marble. His head doesn't turn even a little but a bloom rises in his flawless skin. Her palm sings. She wants to grit her teeth but he will see. "I'm icing out nothing. I'm asking for respect. Girl doesn't like the rules. Doesn't have to follow them."

She rounds the table to get right up against Floro. Only got a half inch on him but she can make it a mile. "Lazy son. You like the roof over your head? You like a dry place to come scratch your balls after a long hard day of doing zero? I can change the locks on you too, how about? Nothing easier."

Floro's mouth cinches up in a bitter knot. His body stays perfectly still and then his fist slams into the table. The cup jumps, tips over. Liquid unfurls across the tabletop. Floro spins away from her, puts as much space between the two of them as the room will allow (which, ha, is not much at all). In front of the far window he stills, leaning against the splintered molding. When he straightens there will be paint flakes on his shoulder. "It's all wrong, Mom."

Offie watches him, the single braid that hangs down his back, the arcs of muscle that breach his neck like the backs of whales. The spilled water creeps cool between her fingers.

Hey everybody, gather round. Put that away, come in, shut the door. Ofelie's going to teach us how to play a game. She takes a black plastic case down from a high shelf by the water tank and walks to the recliner. Back on the futon, Floro sees what she's doing and goes, *Of course,* but doesn't try to stop her.

What's inside the case is three black balls, marble-size. Lighter than you'd expect, polka-dotted all over with little gold connector pins. Where they go is the three tiny wells sunk in Offie's body. Two in the tendony insides of her wrists, one in the back of her neck, just above the first knob of her spine. Crusty little punch-holes that she swabs with rubbing alcohol less often than she should.

Here's the thing about games: they are not an addiction. No, really. You yearn to enter the game world only as much as you yearn to escape this one. It's not that planet calling you. It's this one pushing you away. And hold up there, one more thing: it is not freedom. No matter what you've heard. You take your body with you. Whatever scars you bear, you bear them everywhere.

Leafy shadows sway against the yellow walls of the entry. Offie steps out of her clogs and bears the groceries down the hall to the kitchen.

The kitchen counters are dark granite flecked with mica; the glazed tile backsplash matches the blue of the shutters. She places the vegetables on the countertop by the sink. Asparagus, brussels sprouts, green-and-yellow-streaked tomatoes sitting fat and tender in her hands. String beans, a bouquet of basil. She crushes a leaf and the kitchen air sharpens and clarifies. The sack of corn she leaves bundled on the table. There are three bags of food now, though she only carried one.

Cereal is scattered on the floor by the pantry. Milk puddles make amoeba-like shapes on the floorboards. Someone has been experimenting with snack composition. She rolls her eyes and calls down the hallway. "*Hailo.*" The voice she uses is dredged deliberately from her belly, honed and funneled up until she can aim it precisely as a garden hose toward the ears of her younger daughter.

From somewhere on the second floor comes a shrill reply. "Yeah?"

"Will you come down to the kitchen?"

She receives no confirmation, but detects a faint shuffling of fabric and plastic parts and can picture the girl extricating herself from some elaborate costume. While she waits she puts the milk and butter into the door of the refrigerator. She feels a certain heated twinge—something in between pleasure and anticipation—at the thought of making her daughter clean up the cereal. I am making you responsible, she thinks. Ha! You thought you could make a mess, but instead you will become a better person.

Thonk, thonk, thonk. Out of the kitchen, out of the game world, out of even the pathetic Apartamento Ferdinand. All the way out to the rotten foyer. Thonking up the stairs are two more bodies, Ferdinands #2 and #4. In front: Bello, a suppler version of Floro, his face two years younger, less incongruous. Eyebrows spreading unchecked and jawline still hardening. One arm shoulders a purple flowery backpack, the other reaches back to hook fingers with the smaller hand of: Hailo, baby-baby sister, rightful owner of the backpack. Newly nine, with hand-me-down leggings that end three inches above her ankles. Just beginning to feel desire for things that cannot be handed to her. She flexes her fingerpads against her brother's to test the bone under his flesh, keeps her eyes fixed on the back of his head like he's helping her ascend to heaven.

They pick their way up the dark stairs via smell and memory, absorbing the mildew drip in the air, the stale vapor of old cooking oil. They know to step lightly on the ninth riser. They do not touch the soft places on the walls. Hailo moves in double hops, flipping her hips from side to side, telling Bello, ". . . but like, I can *do* a front round-off. It's not even that *hard*."

When the Ferdinand family encounters unkind observers, it may be noted that Hailo will never be as beautiful as her older, absenter sister. Girl has a forehead too high and a laugh too ricocheting. She will not realize until much later than Celado what traps can be woven from hungry eyes. But Hailo, close your ears to those unkind observers. They know not what they say. Even now, even this minute, skipping in the vacuum left by your sister, you are learning to weave other things.

They come into the room just as Mom is settling back in her chair. Marbles snapped into her nodes. The world draining away like sand through a screen. Bello sees her first thing and inside him some trapdoor goes bang-shut. Hailo—in the middle of "I can probably show you right now, even. It's just like so *easy*"—doesn't even pause in her hop-twisting straight toward Offie. "Hey Mom, hey want to see—"

Bello does a long lunge across the carpet and snags second sister's wrist, snaps her away from the still form of their mother. "Don't!"

Hailo twists against him. "Let go let *go!* I want to show her—" And so he kneels, wraps both arms around her, curls her new long body into his new big one. Warm-breathes into the cloud of her hair.

"*Don't.*"

In the blue-tiled kitchen, Hailo laughs when she sees the spilled cereal. "Well, yeah," she shrugs at her mother. "It's better when you mix up all the kinds." Her grin is awkwardly large and her teeth portend orthodonture. She leaps for the dustpan without being told. "Sorry bout that."

Offie removes a tub of cooked pasta from the refrigerator while Hailo uses three times the necessary paper towels to sop up the milk. She dumps the pasta into a bowl, scans a cabinet with her fingertips to find olive oil, red wine vinegar, white pepper.

"Where's your sister?"

Hailo shrugs. "Out." The world of the game does not stretch much beyond the house. Sometimes characters can be vexingly vague when discussing their whereabouts.

"Do you know when she'll be back?"

Hailo shrugs again. She dances over to the counter where her mother works. Her ankles are wrapped in dozens of fluorescent string-bracelets. With her thumb and forefinger, she pulls fusilli out of the bowl and drops them into her mouth. "She'll probably be back for dinner."

"And your brothers?"

Hailo pours salt onto her palm and licks it off. "Out with Dad."

One a.m., two a.m. Moon creeps up, crests, begins to sink. Mother over the horizon, and now the Ferdinand children lay themselves down to sleep. Like he always does Floro tries to push Hailo to the floor, says she doesn't deserve a bed since she's no longer sharing. Little sister doesn't say a thing, just blanks her face and gives him the wide-eye until he retreats to the other futon with Bello. Everybody has their rituals.

They leave the window open and cold air sweeps their skin through the threadbare sheets. Bello and Floro arrange themselves in a frozen brawl. Fist to cheek, knee to stomach. Since babyhood have they slept like this, double heart, waking with bruises only they can decipher. Hailo drifts on the expanse of futon, tumble-twisting, unmoored. When Celado slept next to her they never touched; Cece always curled on the far edge with her elegant slumber scowl. But still. They sleep, three contorted quarters of a whole, her absence a small puncture in their lungs through which the air whistles.

The last time Celado stood in that room? Yeah sure, went like this: mother and daughter, circling each other with stretched arms like witches raising a spell. Celado, her face so blazing it could have killed you or brought you back to life. Her mane of dark hair snarled back from her head, her ass drooping below short-shorts, her nails bitten down to red moons. Ofelie in her nightgown, face gouged with desperation, trying to smother the fear egg hatching inside her.

"I'm keeping it," Celado said. "Hector loves me."

Offie's eyes could have shattered the windows. "You can't tell love from garbage."

"And who's my teacher?"

"You got a scum brain too."

Flawless teenage shrug. Celado the Bulletproof. "Yeah, well. *My* baby. She's going to know where she comes from."

Offie's voice hoarse with rage: "Out." Offie's voice a whispered plea. "Out."

Celado went with a screech like an eagle. Slammed the door and opened it and slammed it again.

And Hailo, lying under the futon with her face pressed to the pink hippo, thought: this must be what love is. Nobody who didn't love each other could want so badly to eat each other's hearts.

Present night, in the alcove. Offie is a peaceful sculpture of herself. The falling moon drapes strands of light along her nose, the rise of her cheekbone. Look at her now, you would swear, it must be the real world she has vanished to. This place, this cold crowded room, these children who sleep like they've been gunned down, this must be the game world, which she only visits now and then.

She rinses brussels sprouts in the sink, shucking off the outer leaves under a ribbon of water. Through the window above the sink she watches the wide green bowl of her backyard, the patio with gardenias still blooming.

The game always supplies her with a husband. She cannot remember making this request but perhaps it read her unspoken desires. This one is only a pirated version bought from an old co-worker, but still she is often surprised at how it anticipates her.

They do not have sex; it has been nine years and nine months since sex seemed like a good idea. And she sleeps, when she sleeps, on a king-sized bed with a white duvet that is for her and her alone. Rather his presence manifests in tasks accomplished while she is not around. The shutters, for instance, or bunk beds assembled in the girls' room. When it snows, her walk is always shoveled. Sometimes there are flowers for her on the kitchen table. She cannot quite say how she knows this is the work of more than a maintenance script, but she does. He is undoubtedly his own entity.

Occasionally, when she is busy with something like moving laundry, or standing at the sink, he will come up behind her and rest his warm callused hands on the place where her neck meets her shoulders, and her eyes will grow hot with tears.

At work the next day, conveyor belts rurr as always. Offie rustles through rafts of cardboard caked with food, squeegees it away with blue-gloved fingers. Across from her there are no friendly overtures from Silene, not even eye contact. The cool from last night has passed; the air in the warehouse is thick and dull. Offie reaches under the cardboard for something that clatters and comes back mooing in pain. Someone has cast into the stream a bucket of syringes, uncapped. Her blue glove dots with red.

Ah-ah-ah. The claws above her wheeze with laughter. You see, you are no good at this. There is nothing we cannot do better than you.

Twitch, twitch. Offie twitches her shoulders, trying to dislodge the voices from her ears. She jerks her hand once across her face and streaks her temple with blood.

Ah-ah. We can do your job better. We can raise your children better. Your missing, slut-tastic daughter? We could point the way to her immediately. We could even reach out (we are factory-specialized for reaching out, remember) and pluck her from the maelstrom, as easily as we pluck a single styrofoam cup from the flood.

Oh you humans! (The imaginary claws jab Offie's armflesh in a jocular, aggressive way.) Oh-oh, you haven't made a thing yet that we could not pluck out! And when we pluck a thing, it doesn't get away. It goes down exactly the chute it belongs. No matter if it is dirty or crumpled or used up, it goes down the chute and through the fires and gets formed into something new. Something useful. Something better. Perhaps that would be good for your daughter too. We will pluck her up from the dirt-hole where she's hiding, with her latest string-muscle man who likes to stroke his dick across her belly. We will drag her out and drop her down the chute and push her through the fire, and it will burn the vileness out of her, it will melt down her used-up skin-n-bones body, we'll sear the animal out of her, we'll—

NO!

Offie roars like she can blast the thoughts from her mind. She tears at her head with mothereagle talons, wrenches so hard her hand comes away with a hank of hair. Her head rings in the quiet. Blood drips onto her collarbone.

Across from her, Silene makes a micro noise, *a-a*, and collapses forward onto the conveyor belt.

Her body pushes a wave of junk off the belt and onto Offie. Panic, canaries shrieking all down the line. Silene's torso is borne a few feet downstream, legs dragged along behind, and then she *floops!* sideways onto the concrete.

Inside Offie a continent shifts. Maybe her head is still full of the scraping claw laughter, maybe her lungs are still full of her own roar. She pushes the junk heap away, plants a hand, heaves herself onto the belt. In a second she is on the other side, heavy-breathing, kneeling by Silene.

"Hey, hey, girl, girl-o, where are you? Where are you?"

She holds Silene's face in both hands, brushes her gray lips, presses her cheek to Silene's cold forehead. "Water!" Looks up to see the other workers pressed sheeplike together. "You are stupid? Water! Help!"

But the sheep/canaries are pushed aside and Supervisor emerges, guiding a floating stretcher that bumps his side like a nervous dog. "Hurry up, get her to the resus mod, we're losing time."

She thinks he means time to save Silene, but no, duh, he means productivity tracking. Together they roll Silene (like she is full of volcanic sand!) onto the stretcher. It rises, wobbles under her weight, whirrs slowly toward the exit.

Outside the warehouse there is a blue-&-white-striped vehicle, like an ambulance but sleeker. The recycling company parks it there for cases of extreme dehydration (also boneheaded dosings, hunger strikes, et alia). The stretcher whirrs up to it. Offie and Supervisor follow at a distance, Offie sneezing in the sudden daylight. The achy blue above them is a perfect match with the stripes on the resuscitation module. Silene's feet flop back and forth with the motion of the stretcher; one hand drops off and swings like a pendulum. A small door at one end of the module slides up, just high enough for a stretcher bearing a body to slip inside. The stretcher fidgets for a moment, fits itself into the proper grooves, whirrs forward into the smooth white tube. Inch by inch, Silene disappears.

Beside Offie, Supervisor looks pleased. "Ten minutes in there, she'll be fine. Don't worry."

Offie gives him the sharpest side-eye she can. Really, Mister Navid? Really? Suddenly afraid that he will try to pat her on the back, she edges away, then stumps back into the warehouse.

His estimate was off: Silene returns in thirteen minutes. Her lips are still gray but her skin is dry. Her arms move like they are propelled by well-greased pistons.

"Silene. What do they do in there?"

Silene's eyes aren't focusing. She parts her lips a few times before speaking. "I don't remember."

"Truth?" Offie grimaces. She wishes she could switch places with someone farther down the line. Silene's straight back and sharp movements give her the jitters. People should break when they are wounded, don't you think? Offie knows it. People should show their scars.

She shakes as she walks from the bus station, as she climbs the stairs. Again and again she sees Silene collapse like a boneless thing, hears the claws cackle. Her skin feels alive; it is unbearable the way her clothes rest against her body.

No offspring are around when she arrives home. She makes a straight line for the chair. The feeling of fullness within, that calms her without. Why does it not exist in this world? Here she contains only air and grief and cruel voices. She wants it back, she wants it back. Her hands slip as she tries to fit the balls into her nodes and she must retrieve them once, twice, before they are snapped into place. *A-a*. Do you know how the ship feels as it slips over the horizon? No, you say, because to the ship there is no horizon, there is only sailing farther and farther. But there is a feeling (yes, there is!) of watching the known world drop under the ocean. Of knowing you are out of sight, of easier breathing. As the game revs up that feeling seeps warmly through her flesh. Offie, come back! Are you listening? Ofelie, Mama Love-n-Hate, turn around, there's still time—

Around her there is only open sea. Finally, she thinks. Finally. They cannot get me now.

Floro and Bello park their scooters in the street in front of a house. You want precision: in front of the garage of a house. The garage is complete but the house—big fat-man colonial—is only framing, no sheetrock or siding. Its bare beams have slipped down the years from pressure-treated yellow to bloodless gray.

They frown at the closed garage door.

Bello bounces on the balls of his feet. "Sure this is it?"

"Doubting me?" Floro nudges him. "Yeah. *Sure*. I meet the guy Hector a while ago. I *know*." He doesn't say where he met Hector, but if you know the kinds of pursuits Floro engages in, you can guess.

"Kay." Bello shrugs. "Just not looking to start a thing."

They walk up to the garage door. They move like they have not eaten in weeks. Like one of them might be the savior of the world. There's only one person on the whole freaking planet who could possibly be in that garage who should not be afraid.

The door begins to rise and yellow daylight scans across the floor, revealing a garage converted into a makeshift home. Haphazard rugs, a lamp, rageporn posters tacked over unpainted walls. On a bare mattress in the back, cross-legged, still, a person-shape too shadowed to make out. The brothers strain forward. The light slides up her body, reveals the swollen belly she cradles with her hands, the hollows of her face, little dents in her bottom lip where she bites it, gray fairyqueen eyes. Celado Ferdinand.

"You're here." She shakes like a bird pulled from an oil spill. Ready to sink her claws into anyone who gets too close. "Hector's gone. He's gone two days. I think—I think it's for real this time."

Floro sucks his teeth, shakes his head. "You come with us, kid sister." There's nobody who can tell if that's a question or not. Probs Floro isn't sure, but he doesn't leave things to chance. He walks into the garage, all the while secret-like planning what he will do to Hector, whom he knows from certain pursuits, which limbs he will rend first.

They pull her up, hold her among their four arms. They remember when she was born, how Offie dipped her into their laps for seconds at a time. *Be careful with the baby!* Bello lets his hand hover a millimeter above her stomach. "How far along?"

That makes her smile. "Six months." She traces shapes around her belly button. "Almost a real person now."

They do not know what to make of this. Not afraid but of course afraid. Bello nudges her shoulder with his. "Can you ride the scooter with me? Back to Colt's Brook?"

Celado chews her lip. "I think so." Her smile shrinks. "She doesn't want me there."

"She's out twenty-four seven without you. Everything falls apart."

Standing as she is, the light hits her torso but leaves her face dark. Celado puts a hand on each brother's shoulder, feels the play of their muscles under skin. There are vast countries in them that are alien to her, and then there are these small points of contact. On the edges of their sweat she smells the mustyrot of home.

(How did you do it, Cece? Call out to them over the cul-de-sacked void. Summon them to your unlocked garage door. What everybody should know is, this is the particular gift/curse of the Ferdinand kids. In their hours of need, they can conjure up rescue. They can make something from nothing. Fire from the airless dark. Shaking love from still flesh. Spoiler alert: this is gonna be their doom, also. All that power, what do you think they do? Burn things, burn each other, burn themselves all down. Celado, do you really think you're being saved right now? Does anyone?)

She says, "Kay."

The house is silent, empty when Hailo gets home from school. To check she does cartwheels from one side of the room to the other. She walks on her hands by the boxes of commodity food. She does a headstand on the futon and stomps her sneakers against the wall. No one says Ai watch out, or Get the fuck outside, or Ow that was my head! Really truly authentically empty room.

Except not empty, of course: there is Offie in her chair, quiet statue of maternity.

Hailo carries her backpack over to Offie, lays it on the floor at mama's feet. "See what I do in school today, Mom?" Picks out folded paper shapes, a wheelie car, a whale, a crane. "I learn how to make all these." She arranges them in a parade up Offie's stomach. "I'm doing real good in all the subjects." She sits on the floor with her knees twisted up and her back resting against Offie's shins. Tilts her head gently to lay it in Offie's lap. "I'm gonna get the fuck out of here." In Hailo's ear comes the murky tidal whisper of Offie's pulse. Against Hailo's cheek, mama's thigh is warm.

At the kitchen table, Offie teaches Hailo to snap asparagus. She shows her how to grip the chunky white end and bow the green flower down. "Each stalk knows where to break. That's how you make sure you get all of the sweet part, and none of the woody part."

Hailo wrinkles her nose. "I don't even like asparagus." She continues to snap the stalks. "It makes my pee smell funny."

Offie laughs. "It makes everyone's pee smell funny. Some people even like the smell."

Hailo is so repulsed by this that she has to cease her snapping and push the bowl away. Offie gives her sugar peas to shell instead. Hailo fills her mouth with sweet green beads and watches her mother thoughtfully.

"I got a question for you."

Offie arranges the asparagus in a roasting pan. "Yes?"

"How come you go away sometimes?"

Offie doesn't miss a beat as she pours olive oil. "What do you mean?"

"Ughhh. Come on. You know."

She shuffles the asparagus spears in the oil. "Well. There's just more than one place I have to be."

"I miss you, when you go away."

She slides the pan into the oven and goes back to where Hailo sits. With her thumbs, she smooths her daughter's hair from her face and brushes a pea fragment from her lip. She kneels so she is eye level with the girl. "I know, sweetheart.

I know. I would stay here forever if I could. Sometimes you can't . . ." Uncertain where to go from here, she leans forward to envelop Hailo in her arms. The girl's hair tickles her nose. "Can you remember this for me? It is possible for a person to love and be hungry at the same time. It doesn't make either of them hurt any less."

Hailo submits to the hug docilely, neither pulling away nor reciprocating.

They make it down the highway, Celado on the scooter barnacled to Bello's back. They make it to the neighborhood, past the curliqued Colt's Brook Estate sign. With every bum no one who *Hey-yahs* out as they pass, Celado tightens to a brittler and brittler knot. They make it into the sad identical house, through the foyer, halfway up the creaking stairs, Cece leading with Bello/Floro trailing her like an honor guard. Then she freezes. Her fingers redden around the banister. Chest starts heaving like she's oxygenating a bonfire.

"I can't." Not going to do it. Nu-uh, sorry, no way no how. "She hates me."

Quick, Floro/Bello, into damage-control mode. "No she doesn't," "Cece, come on," "You're so close!"

"*Nnnn!*" She makes a wild noise and flips around to face the two of them. Gutter growl: "She calls me *garbage*." Fear churns hateful possibilities through her head. "You don't *care*! You just want me there so she steps off *you!*"

The plan is slipping, it's going wrong. They want to fix it but also they are angry at her for messing it up. Can't ever admit it, princes of chaos that they are, but all they want is for things to be as they were. Both sisters safe-n-sound, Mom in the waking world. They see so clearly how the world could be righted. Why can't someone, for once, do what they want? Why can't she? Why does she have to be so stubborn, so vile?

Celado sees them coming up at her, grim-faced, hands outstretched. And in that second, Cece, you understand it in your bones: you are their sister, you are just one more thing they can seize. They can drop you down any chute they want.

Shrieking time is over, she just does a single quiet sob, clutches the bannister tighter, curls into the wall. And feels pain shaft through her abdomen. Her whole body shudders. Floro and Bello freeze. And then she is only rays of pain, filling her body like light, and she forgets to clutch anything. She is a star falling in slow-mo. Her brothers' hands open, no longer to grab but to catch. Just in time. She tumbles against them and their knotty palms feel soft, soft as clouds.

Offie's conversation with Hailo is interrupted by a storm of noise in the front hallway. The boys must be home. She calls to them to clean their shoes off but she cannot tell if it makes any impact. The yelling continues, and there is a clatter as though someone has stumbled on the stairway. She cannot imagine what the problem could be, but she is glad they are back because she needs help carrying plates to the table in the backyard. As she heads toward the door something in the game air tugs at her. It is as though a clammy hand has grazed her wrist. Or perhaps a spiderweb has caught along her jaw. She brushes her arms absently.

Without warning, Floro's face appears right up against her own. He is yelling, but she cannot make out the words. It is as though he calls to her from under fathoms of water. Bello she sees also, slightly behind Floro, his arms flailing and his face in spasms, but he neither makes any sound. Just as quickly as they confronted her, both of her sons melt away. She pivots back to the kitchen in irritation. It would be so much better if they would just tell her what was going on. It was always a joke, keeping Mom in the dark. She will not rise to their bait; they can come to her if they wish. Right now she needs to put the corn on the grill.

Hailo is sunk in a doze when the door bangs open; she leaps away from Offie with a yelp. Her brothers, propping up something between them—some*one*—her *sister*. Hailo yelps again. Not sure whether to run to them or flatten herself against the wall. She trips on nothing and catches herself. Yelps again.

The boys ease Celado down on the futon. Her huge belly convulses, her legs jerk back and forth. Looks like she's seizuring but actually she's just shaking her head back and forth, denying the whole world with a barely there voice. "No, no, no, no, no." Her skintight shorts are dark with liquid; it shines on her thighs and soaks into the couch.

"Shit," Floro says. "Shit. *Shit.*"

Bello is silent. Wraps his arms around his abdomen then clutches his neck then runs hands through his hair then back to his stomach. He catches sight of Hailo.

"Wake Mom up!"

"What? But it's danger—"

"Doesn't matter." He points to Celado. "She needs the hospital."

Celado's nos dissolve into moans now, rhythmic, warlike. Her eyes stare into the in-between.

Hailo gentle-pokes Offie in the neck. "Mom?"

No response.

Floro pushes her out of the way. "Let me do it."

Offie's face is serene. Her eyeballs scan and twitch under their lids. Floro slaps her hard across the face, WHACK. Like slapping raw meat. Her head snaps to the side. For a second her eyelids fly open and Hailo sees her whole irises, two gray orbs ringed with straining white. Gray like her children's eyes. Her children who stand before her, fragmented with desperation. Savers of small things, remakers of the world. She sees them for a second, or she doesn't.

Her eyes fall shut.

Floro loses it, up in her face, voice growing deranged: "Mom, Mom, wake the fuck up, *Mom, Mom, Mom!*"

Bello, kneeling by first-sister: "Hit her again."

Hailo watches Floro raise his arm again and swing, hears the raw meat noise, feels her own flesh flash with pain. Nothing.

Floro inhales hard through his nose. Bello still bent prayer-style over Celado. Hailo clenches her face, squeezes back tears, feels the silent-winged approach of a moment that will leave nothing unchanged.

"*Again.*"

There! The patio table is set. The corn is grilling, and she has set out crumbled cheese, mayonnaise, and chili powder in which to roll the cobs. There is pasta salad, roasted asparagus, the swollen tomatoes sliced and layered with basil and mozzarella. Her sons are bearing chairs out from the kitchen. Hailo has a glittery hula hoop and is running in the grass, jerking her head like a starving bird to keep it rotating around her neck. Offie feels her brain turn yet again to her one absent daughter. Celado must be home in time. Then everything will be as it should.

The sun is halfway to setting and the air hints at the tang of autumn. Above the horizon there is a band of clear orange sky, and above that a single enormous cloud stretches overhead. Offie raises her eyes and is struck by the sensation of standing on the seafloor, looking up through the depths at the bottom of a ship as large as the whole Earth. Its hull curves from pole to pole, burning with the vanished sun, murky blue shot through with pink and purple.

Hailo gives a shout and tosses her hoop high in the air. Celado is home. Ofelie looks toward the edge of the yard and sees a slender silhouette at the top of the hill. Her older daughter, dark against the blazing sky, her outline bleeding into the sunset.

Joy floods through her. "Cece, look!" She points enthusiastically at the table. "Corn de elote!"

Celado starts down to the house. Ofelie watches her with a gentleness that condenses into a sting. Her vision blurs for a moment, and as it clears she notices motion on the hill behind her daughter. With a faint rippling of the grass, more silhouettes appear on the crest. They are smaller than Celado, with spindly legs and bobbing heads. First there are three, then seven, then their numbers grow too quickly to be counted. Celado, skipping forward, does not seem to notice. Around her the grass shifts. The hill is cracking like skin. More small figures emerge from the cracks, pulling themselves up with stick arms.

The air is perfect, barely felt, but Offie shivers. Celado is almost here; soon she will be close enough to discern her expression. The light shifts. Above them the huge cloud-ship begins to fragment. Electric pink scabs peel off the sky. Through the gaps spindly feet drop down, kicking wildly, searching for purchase on the air. The figures lower themselves through the cloud as though through a trapdoor, and let go.

Offie's mouth has dropped open in a shape of helplessness and she pulls it back into a smile. There is no reason to despair. The table is set. The chairs will be full. Around her, wobbly figures drop from the air, heave themselves up from the earth, stumble toward her home. The ground is roiling, bubbling up. The sky is nearly gone. Her head spins; she feels like she is falling from a great height and yet not moving. She gasps and it comes out as laughter. Of course they would all make it in time. How ridiculous, the amount of relief she feels. She was so worried, but it is okay. Everything is coming back to her now.

Acknowledgments

For the immense effort of material and imaginative collaboration that any book represents, thanks go out:

To Small Beer Press—Kelly Link and Gavin J. Grant—unparalleled examples of how to bring worlds onto the page, and pages into the world. Who saw what I most wanted to be seen and offered to make it real. And Paul Witcover and Te Chao for the gift of a breathtaking book object.

To my agent, Kristina Moore, who convinced me that this book could exist out in the world.

To my mentors at Oberlin: Sylvia Watanabe, Lynn Powell, and Dan Chaon, for the gifts of close scrutiny and generosity that extended far beyond the classroom.

To my faculty and cohort at the Clarion West Writers Workshop, with whom so many of these stories were born.

To my Michener teachers for your astonishing support—Jim Magnuson, Kirk Lynn, Steven Dietz. To Elizabeth McCracken for modelling art-making and teaching and living with a grace I can only hope to aspire to.

To my Michener family: David Semonchik who I'll always be writing for, Sam Sax, Lydia Blaisdell, Rachel Kondo, Bing Li, Fatima Kola, Maya Perez, Sam Miller, Scott Guild, and everyone who lifted me through the grad school years and showed me what a writing community could be.

To my DC family of troublemakers and queers and teachers and organizers carving out vibrant life on the margins of a Dead City—API Resistance; the Full Moon Farmhouse; the DC Creative Writing Workshop, especially Nancy Schwalb, Renita Williams, and the students, before whose writing I will always be humbled.

To my Monkeywrench family for all the other worlds we made possible, late at night on the brink of ruin. For teaching me to trust chaos and move like water.

To everyone whose love and friendship have profoundly shaped me and so shaped the stories I have to tell. Paige Clifton-Steele, Hannah Weiss, Rachel Slezak, Anna Betzel, Sarah Hoops, Keithlee Spangler, Janet Fiskio, Lauren Dixon. Alex Vargo even though she doesn't have a choice about being my friend because she's also my cousin. Corinne Teed for being the first person to hold this book in her hands and read it all the way through.

To everyone unnamed or unseen whose labor has nevertheless helped carry me to this point. To the writers and scholars and revolutionaries who have helped me grapple with what it means to live this science fictional reality, as a mixed-race immigrant settler in the twilight of a colonial empire in the midst of a great extinction.

And to my actual family, who has been willing to share me with all these alien worlds and still always welcome me home. Jesse Bear, obnoxious little brother and the best human I know. My mom who has read everything I ever wrote and always looks up with concern at the end to ask, "But where did that come from?" Who taught me to take risks and get muddy and know the trees by name. My dad who spend endless nights reading aloud to me as a child. Who gave me the gifts of Earthsea and Middle-earth and Pern and Arrakis, and made me want to do it too.

Publication History

These stories were previously published as follows:

"Alien Virus Love Disaster," *StoryQuarterly* 48, 2015
"Blood, Blood," *Strange Horizons,* 2010
"If You Could Be God of Anything" as "Party Doll Surprise Attack," *Abundant Grace: A Collection of Fiction by Washington Area Women,* 2016
"Moonkids," *Explosion Proof Magazine* 5, 2012
"Rich People" (in a slightly different form), *Tin House,* 76, 2018
"Sex Dungeons for Sad People" as "All You Sad People Come Into My Dungeon," *Superficial Flesh,* 2014
"Sweetheart," Tor.com, 2010
"Teacher," *Barrelhouse* 13, 2014
"I'm Sorry Your Daughter Got Eaten by a Cougar," "If You Lived Here, You'd Be Evicted by Now," "Not an Alien Story," and "Ultimate Housekeeping Megathrill 4" are published here for the first time.

About the Author

Abbey Mei Otis is a writer, a teaching artist, a storyteller, and a firestarter raised in the woods of North Carolina. She loves people and art forms on the margins. She studied at the Michener Center for Writers in Austin, TX, and the Clarion West Writers Workshop, and now teaches at Oberlin College in Ohio. Her stories have recently appeared in journals including *Tin House, StoryQuarterly, Barrelhouse,* and Tor.com.